R my name is Rosie

R my name is Rosie

Barbara Cohen

Lothrop, Lee & Shepard Company
A Division of William Morrow & Company, Inc.
New York

Books by Barbara Cohen

Benny
The Binding of Isaac
Bitter Herbs and Honey
The Carp in the Bathtub
R My Name Is Rosie
Thank You, Jackie Robinson
Where's Florrie?

First Edition
1   2   3   4   5   6   7   8   9   10

Library of Congress Cataloging in Publication Data

Cohen, Barbara.
    R, my name is Rosie.

    SUMMARY: Feeling neglected by her innkeeper mother, Rosie reveals her feelings and dreams in a fantasy world called the Land of Three Roses which she and her bartender friend create together.
    [1. Single-parent family—Fiction. 2. Hotels, motels, etc.—Fiction]
I. Title.
PZ7.C6595Rac   [Fic]   77-28867
ISBN 0-688-41839-2
ISBN 0-688-51839-7 lib. bdg.

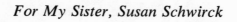

For My Sister, Susan Schwirck

A rose is a rose is a rose.

Rachel said that to me all the time. I didn't know what it meant. It was from some writer. Rachel was always talking about some writer. I tried to keep up, but I wasn't all that interested. Rachel and I are much less alike than she thinks. We care about different things. Her favorite book is *Jane Eyre;* mine is *The Wind in the Willows.*

But I needed Rachel. There was so much I didn't know. For example, I didn't know what went with what. I knew there were rules about those things. I just didn't know what the rules were. One morning when Rachel came into my room, I was standing in front of my closet, trying to decide what blouse to wear with what skirt. I did that every morning.

7

Right away Rachel began to yell. "My God, it's almost seven-thirty and you're still in your pajamas. You're going to be late to school again."

"I don't know what to wear," I told her. "I can't decide."

"My God!" she cried again, in exasperation. She came over to the closet and grabbed a gray skirt off its hanger. Then she opened my drawer and pulled out a light blue angora sweater. She threw them both on my bed. "Wear these," she said.

"They go together?"

"Of course they go together. Would I pick them out for you to wear if they didn't go together?"

"Blue and gray?"

"Blue and gray go together beautifully."

"OK." Now at last I was sure. Now I knew two colors that definitely went with each other. I'd wear that gray flannel skirt and blue angora sweater to school every single day if I had to, just to be safe.

"I'll braid your hair," Rachel offered.

I didn't want her to do that. "You do a lousy job," I said. "I want Mom to do it. When you do it, it's lopsided all day."

"Well, then, don't braid it. Wear it loose, if you insist. But don't wake up Mother. The volunteer fire company had a banquet last night and I'm sure she couldn't close the Inn before two in the morning."

I wanted to wake Mom up. She'd fix my hair with her eyes half-shut, and I'd end up with braids even more lopsided than the ones Rachel made, but I didn't care. I just wanted to see her, that's all. "Listen, Rachel," I said, "I don't feel too good. I've got a stomach ache. I think I'll stay home today."

"Oh, no, you won't," Rachel said, making a face. She had a whole collection of faces. She could look kind, like the bear in "Snow White and Rose Red," or sad and overworked, like the horse in *Black Beauty,* or intelligent and capable, like dogs in books by Albert Payson Terhune. Right now she looked like the Wicked Witch of the West. "There isn't a thing wrong with you," she scolded, "and you'll go to school just like you're supposed to. My God, you haven't gone to school five consecutive days since you hit second grade." I was now in fifth grade. If Rachel was right, I had missed about a hundred days of school. That wasn't really possible, was it?

"How do you know what my stomach feels like?" I asked her. "If it's better later, Mom can take me to school when she gets up."

Rachel stared at me. I could tell she was thinking. She picked up the blue angora sweater from the bed. "Is this the sweater Aunt Faye sent you for your birthday?" I nodded. "The one that came from Best's?" I nodded again. Aunt Faye was very rich. The only things I got from Best's were what she sent me for my birthday and Christmas. Aunt Faye celebrated Christmas, even though she was Jewish, like us. I was glad she did. The things Aunt Faye gave me were the only brand-new clothes I had. Everything else was a hand-me-down from Rachel. Before that, they were hand-me-downs to Rachel from Aunt Faye's daughter, Cousin Stephanie. There was one trouble with stuff from Best's—it never wore out.

Rachel held the sweater up against her chest and looked at herself in the mirror. "I think this would probably fit me. I bet it's too big for you anyway. I think I'll wear it today. You won't mind, because you're not going to school. You won't even dress until Mother gets up and makes you. You'll walk around until noon in your bathrobe."

I grabbed the sweater out of her hand and put it on right over my pajamas. It was a trick. Rachel was always playing tricks on us, getting us to do things we didn't want to do. I couldn't help that now. I meant to wear that blue sweater myself. Finally I knew what to wear it with. I was going to go to school in it, and I was going to look as good as Millie Van Dyke or Cheryl Crane. I didn't want Rachel stretching it out of shape. She always ate breakfast with her nose in a book. She might slob my sweater up with egg yolk. "All right," I said. "All right. I'll go to school. If I throw up in the middle of arithmetic, it'll be your fault."

"OK," Rachel agreed, "it'll be my fault. I'm going down now to make breakfast. Don't forget to wake up Dan before you come down."

"Do I have to? He'll yell at me again. I wish you'd wake him. He doesn't yell at you so much."

"Oh, yes, he does," she said. "Anyway, waking him up is your job. Making breakfast is my job; waking Dan is your job."

"And what's Dan's job?" I asked.

"Humph," Rachel kind of grunted. "That's a good question." She didn't stay to discuss it, however. She grabbed her school books and marched out the door.

I dressed in the gray skirt and blue sweater, and I went to Dan's room. I slept in room #2 of our Inn; he slept in room #1. The rooms were connected, but I had to go out into the hall to get to his. He always kept the door between our two rooms locked from his side. He didn't keep the door to the hall locked, though. Mom wouldn't let us lock our doors. She liked to come into our rooms before she went to bed to make sure we were all right. That's what she said, but I don't know if she really did it. I never saw her in the middle of the night, except if I was really sick, or something like that.

I pushed the door open and went into Dan's room. His walls were completely covered with pictures of baseball players. He'd cut them out of the Sunday *News* and *Baseball* and *Sport* magazines. He'd hung up a few jazz musicians too. The only place in his room you could see the color of the paint was the ceiling. Even that was all spotted with black marks, from his softball. He spent hours lying in bed, listening to ball games on the radio and throwing that ball against the ceiling.

I couldn't see his face. The covers were pulled up

over his head. All there was of him was a lump in the bed, which I shook. "Wake up, Dan," I said as loud as I could. "Wake up." You couldn't be gentle with Dan. I was shouting loud enough to wake up whoever was sleeping across the hall in room #5, but Dan didn't even move.

I pulled the covers off his sleeping body. That did it. He turned over and opened one eye. Then he shut it again. "Wake up," I repeated. He groaned. Maybe his groan sounded something like, "OK, OK," but I knew I couldn't count on it. "Sit up in bed," I shouted. "Sit up and say, 'I'm awake.' " I had to make him do that. If I didn't wake him all the way, he'd be late for school. Then at night, he'd have a big fight with me. He'd end up throwing me on the floor and sitting on top of me. I tugged at his arms. "Come on," I said. "Get up."

I finally got him to sit up. "I'm awake," he said, quite clearly.

"Breakfast is ready," I said. "It's ready *now*." It wasn't, but that's what I had to say.

"Shut the window," he grumbled. "It's cold in here."

His room was small, but it had three windows in a bow in front. There was a big one in the middle and two smaller ones on either side. I wished I had that bow in my room. I went over and shut the window that was open, the one on the right. I peered down the long gravel drive which led from the Waterbridge Inn to the highway. I wanted to see Minnie's old Model T crawling up the drive. Minnie was the waitress who'd

12

worked for my mother the longest. Maybe she was coming to work early, for some reason or other. If she were, *she* could braid my hair.

Of course, I really wanted Mom to braid my hair. I thought it would be nice to have a mother who didn't work. Or if she had to work, she could work in some office, and we could all live in a regular house, or even an apartment, instead of an inn. And then she'd be all done with work by five o'clock in the afternoon. A mother like that would be up in the morning to braid your hair and make your breakfast. My mother never was. I had to settle for Min early in the morning. Min was short and fat, like a barrel. Even though she was forty at least, she wore her dyed red hair piled in curls on top of her head, and huge bright enamelled flower clips in her ears. I loved her and she loved me, but she wasn't my mother. And that particular morning, I didn't even see Min.

I knew I'd better get moving, or Rachel's prediction would come true and I'd be late for school. Dan was sitting on the edge of his bed, his bare, skinny legs dangling to the floor. "Hurry up," I said as I left his room. "Breakfast will be cold."

Then I went down to the Holiday Room to eat. Though the tables had been cleared after the fire company's banquet the night before, the smell of stale cigarette smoke and flat beer still hung over the room. I sat down at the bare wooden table next to the kitchen door where the family and the help always took their meals. Rachel came in through the swinging doors from the kitchen. She was carrying a tray with three plates of fried eggs, a basket of toast, a bowl with three oranges in it, and three cups of cocoa.

We didn't say much to each other as we started in on our breakfast. Rachel and I were halfway through when Dan showed up. Rachel didn't even look up from her book when he came in. She and I kept on eating, but Dan just sat in his chair, staring at the food.

Finally Rachel looked up. "Eat your breakfast," she ordered, and then she turned back to the page in front of her.

"I can't," Dan replied.

Rachel looked up again. "You have to," she said. "Dr. Krause told Mother you're too thin." Dan was just the opposite of Rachel and me.

"The eggs are hard," Dan said. "The cocoa has skin on it. The toast is cold."

"Do you expect me to stand around in the kitchen, waiting for you to come down before I cook the food?" Rachel asked sarcastically. She looked like the Wicked Witch of the West again. "If I did that, I'd never get a chance to eat my own breakfast. I'm not your servant, you know."

Dan let up on Rachel and started in on me. "Why didn't you wake me up on time?" he asked. "If you got me up on time, I'd get down here before the breakfast was ruined."

"You're lousy," I told him. "You're the lousiest

person I know. I go in there and I scream and I yell and I pull you around, and you still don't wake up. Is that my fault? Why don't you go to sleep on time, instead of lying around until two in the morning listening to baseball games from St. Louis?"

Dan got up from the table. "Boy, you're stupid," he said. "You don't even know the baseball season's been over for weeks." He threw his napkin down on the table. "I'm getting out of here. Even school is better than this dump." He turned and walked toward the door.

I got up too and ran after him. "Wait for me," I said. "I'm going now too." I certainly didn't feel like walking to school alone. Rachel went to the high school and she didn't start out for another twenty minutes. Dan went to the grammar school, like me, only he was in the eighth grade.

"You can walk with me as far as River Street," Dan said. "After that you have to walk at least one half block behind me." He didn't like me walking with him after he met the guys. Well, that was OK with me. Walking halfway with him was better than walking the whole way alone.

On my way upstairs to brush out my hair and get my books and coat, I met Major Dunleigh. He was taking Mrs. Dunleigh's Boston terrier, Buster, out for his morning walk. "Good morning, Rosie," Major Dunleigh said.

"Good morning, Major Dunleigh," I replied po-

15

litely. I was always as nice as I could be to Major and Mrs. Dunleigh. They lived in room #17, which was the best room in the Waterbridge Inn, and the only one with a private bath. I didn't care about the Dunleighs so much, but I liked Buster, even if he was about ten years old and couldn't run anymore because he had asthma. The Major could take Buster or leave him, but Mrs. Dunleigh adored him. She carried a roll of toilet paper around in her pocketbook so she could wipe his rear end when he came in from doing his business.

"I'm glad I ran into you before you left for school, Rosie," the Major said. "Mrs. Dunleigh doesn't feel too well today, and I have to go into the city. Perhaps you'd walk Buster for her when you come back from school. I'll give you a quarter if you'll do it."

"Oh, you don't have to give me anything," I said. "I'd be glad to do it for nothing. I like Buster." Taking Buster out for a walk all by myself would be a little bit like having my own dog. It certainly wasn't anything anyone had to pay me to do.

"I'd like to pay you," Major Dunleigh said. "Then I'll feel free to ask you again."

I didn't argue with him. I could always use the money.

I got my things together as fast as I could because I knew Dan wouldn't hesitate to leave without me if I took too long. I met him in the lobby and he led the way through the swinging doors, down the marble steps

16

of the foyer, and out onto the long gravel drive.

"I'm going to take Buster for his walk after school," I told him. "The Major said he'd pay me twenty-five cents to do it."

"I wouldn't wipe a dog's rear end for twenty-five dollars," Dan said.

"Oh, I don't think I'll have to do that," I said. "I think Mrs. Dunleigh will do that after I bring him in. Anyway, I wouldn't mind. I can pretend Buster is mine for a little while. Boy, do I wish I had a dog."

" 'An inn is no place for a dog,' " Dan said, exactly mimicking Mom's tone of voice.

"Yeah," I agreed, "no place for *my* dog. It's all right for a customer's dog, like Buster."

"Buster isn't really a dog," Dan explained. "He's so small that in Ma's mind, he doesn't really count. What do you need a dog for, anyway?"

We were standing on the edge of the highway, watching one early morning truck after another screech by. We waited for five minutes before there was a pause in the traffic so we could tear across at sixty miles an hour. "This is why I need a dog," I said. "I'm lonesome. Mom's busy all the time. Maybe it would have been different if Daddy hadn't died, but he did. Rachel has her books. You've got your friends, and baseball and music. But what have I got? The girls I know aren't allowed to cross this highway. They're too young. And I can't go to their houses either, at least not in the

17

winter, because Mom won't let me cross the highway after dark. That's why I need a dog. I'm lonesome. I don't have any friends."

"That's a lot of baloney!" Dan said. "If I look out the window while you're having recess, I always see you in the middle of a whole bunch. And at the Inn, cripes, Min is always fussing with your hair, or Tex is gabbing with you while he polishes glasses behind the bar."

"Grown-ups don't count as friends," I told him. He knew that. "As for those playground people, they're not friends either. Millie Van Dyke hasn't talked about anything for the last week except her birthday party. She went on and on about it right in front of me, and she didn't even invite me. Now, why is that? What's the matter with me?"

"You're kind of fat," Dan said flatly, "and a lot of the time your braids are crooked."

"Yeah," I agreed, "I know." I felt like crying, but I didn't. Dan got almost as mad at me as Mom did when I cried.

"But," Dan went on, "that's not why Millie Van Dyke didn't invite you to her party. She's a stuck-up snob, that's why. Her brother Carl called me a dirty Jew yesterday."

"What did you do?" I wanted to know. For a minute I forgot about my own problems. Dan's was more interesting. "You couldn't hit Carl. He's twice as big as you are."

"I told him to shut his fat trap," Dan said, a satisfied

smile on his face. "And Carl said, 'Who's gonna make me?' and Bruce said, 'I am,' so Carl shut up, because he may be twice as big as me, but Bruce is twice as big as him. It was a gas, really. A lot of what goes on in this burg is a gas, if you can manage to see it that way."

We crossed Duval Avenue. Pretty soon Bruce and Gary would be coming down River Street. "OK, now," Dan said. "You stop here and let me go on ahead. I'll be running into the guys any minute."

I didn't argue with him. If I did, the next day he wouldn't walk with me even halfway. I just stopped dead in the middle of the sidewalk while he ran on. When he got to the corner, he turned around and looked at me. I thought for a minute he was going to call to me, and tell me I could walk with him after all. But he didn't. A few seconds later, Bruce and Gary met him and they walked on to school together. I followed almost a block behind, but Dan didn't know it. He never turned around again to look.

At recess later that morning, I ignored Millie Van Dyke, Cheryl Crane, and all that crowd. I was better at "A my name is Anna" than any one of them. Usually I got up to "T my name is Tina" before I missed. But they weren't inviting me to their parties, so I wasn't playing with them.

I stood on the walk in front of the side entrance and played by myself. The other girls were around the corner of the building. They couldn't even see me. In front of me, three boys from my class were shooting baskets. I knew one of them pretty well because he sat behind me. His name was Bart Flint. He was always borrowing my eraser or pestering me for answers to arithmetic problems. He and Jackie and Chris were too short to get the ball in the basket more than once out of twenty tries. After a while, Bart got tired of the whole thing. He walked over to me. "You wanna play catch?" he asked.

"Sure," I said. If I practiced with Bart, maybe I'd get good enough so Dan would play with me sometimes. For a while, we threw my ball back and forth. Then Chris and Jackie quit playing basketball, too. Jackie went off somewhere with the basketball. Chris joined us. We played Monkey-in-the-Middle. I knew the only reason they played with me was because it was my ball. Mostly I was stuck in the middle, but that was all right. At least I was playing.

I felt awful lonesome when school let out. Just about every other girl in the class went off to Millie's party, except Mary Elizabeth Lassiter, who was a freak. I was galumping along home by myself when I heard someone calling me. It didn't sound like Dan. He never walked home with me anyway. I turned around and saw Bart running up Queen street. "I'll walk with you," he managed to say when he caught up to me, all out of breath. He lived three blocks before the highway, right on my way home. But he had never walked with me before.

"You're not going to Millie's party, huh?" he said.

"That's right. I'm not going."

"Why not?" he asked.

What was the matter with him? Was he a moron or something? "I wasn't invited," I said.

"Neither was I," he said.

"So what?" I said. "No boys were."

"What difference does it make to you if you were invited or not?" he asked. "You can have ice cream and cake whenever you want, can't you?"

Did he think the important thing about birthday parties was ice cream and cake? He really was a moron. "I could come with you," he said, "and we could have some ice cream and cake right now."

"OK," I said. "Then we could play ball some more."

"Yeah," he agreed. "After the ice cream and cake."

"Will your mother mind if you cross the highway?" I asked.

"I'm eleven years old," he said. "I guess I can cross an old highway if I want to."

We dashed across the road, and walked up the drive, kicking pebbles as we went. "Boy, it's big, isn't it?" Bart said. I was surprised. The Inn had never seemed big to me. It was just where I lived. I looked up at it. Well, maybe it was big—a big yellow stucco building with red and white striped awnings and monster neon signs on the roof that said "WATERBRIDGE INN." One letter or another of those signs was always out of whack. Once the sign on the right had read "ATE BRID E," while the other had said "AT RIDGE INN." The electrician had to come every other week to get the signs working again. He messed around with the wires in the attic and climbed all over the letters, and still the signs would be right only for a week or two. Mom was always saying she was going to get rid of them, but she never did. Even with half the letters out, you could see those signs five miles down the highway.

When we got inside the building, I dropped my books behind the registration desk. Bart didn't have any. I led him into the kitchen. Luke, the chef, was behind the baking table, rolling out pies. "Hello, Rosie, honey," he said. "Who's your boyfriend?"

"He's not my boyfriend," I said. "He's Bart."

"Sorry, honey," Luke apologized. "Not your boyfriend. Just your friend."

"Yes," I said. "He wants some ice cream and cake."

Luke wiped his floury hand on his apron. "I haven't got any cake," he said. "Will a piece of apple pie do?"

"Sure," Bart said. "That'll do fine. With a lot of vanilla ice cream."

"How about you, honey?" Luke asked me. "You want a piece of apple pie, too?"

"OK," I said. "A small piece. No ice cream."

Pedro, the salad man, wasn't in yet, so Luke went over to the salad bench himself. He gave me a small piece of pie. Then he sliced a big piece for Bart and dipped two huge globs of ice cream on top of it. Bart's tongue licked his lips as he carried his plate into the banquet room. We sat at the family table while I

22

watched him eat that pile of food. "Boy, are you lucky," he said. "You can have all the ice cream you want whenever you want it."

"If you think my mother lets me eat ice cream all day long," I said, "you're crazy. She doesn't let me eat whatever I want, any more than your mother lets you eat whatever you want." Actually, Mom had never said anything about ice cream to me, one way or the other.

When Bart was finished, I said, "Let's go outside and play now."

"Nah," he said. "I want to look around this place a little."

So I showed him around. He had already seen the kitchen, the lobby, and the Holiday Room, which was the name Mom had given the big dining room used for banquets and parties. I took him upstairs and showed him my room, and Dan's and Rachel's. He wanted to see the other ones, where the guests stayed, too. I didn't feel like running back downstairs to get the keys. "Regulars live in some of them," I said. "It's not nice to go into rooms other people live in, except to clean them and change the linen. There are seventeen of them altogether, and you've seen three. That's enough."

"But that one says #18," Bart noted, pointing to the door we were standing next to, the door to my mother's room. "How can that be, if there are only seventeen rooms?"

"There's no #13," I explained. "People are superstitious. No one wants to sleep in a room numbered

13." Then I took him downstairs, into the Colonial Room. That was what my mother called the restaurant part, where people came for lunch and dinner. Next to it was the bar room, lined with blue mirrors. The bar was a big semicircle upholstered in blue leather. A bunch of chrome bar stools stood around it. Blue leather banquettes with blue and chrome tables hugged the walls. A piano, a Hammond organ, and a TV set stood on a small platform behind the bar. A lot of people had TV sets now. Two years ago, when Mom had bought one for the bar, they were a novelty. People came to bars just to watch TV. We had seen TV every day, long before other kids—except for very rich ones, like Dan's friend Gary.

Tex the bartender was alone in the bar, polishing glasses. Every afternoon Tex polished glasses. He dusted the bottles on the back bar. He oiled the wooden surface of the bar top. "Hiya, Princess," he said when he saw me. "Who's your buddy?"

"This is Bart," I said.

"Could I have a Coke?" Bart asked.

I was surprised. I didn't see how he could swallow another thing. "Aren't you afraid you'll get sick?" I asked him.

"Nah," he said, "not me." He scooped a handful of peanuts out of the silver bowl on the bar. "I never get sick."

"Sure you can have a Coke," Tex said. "What do you want, Princess?"

24

"Nothing, thanks," I told him. Tex drew a Coke from the tap and put it up on the bar. Bart drank it down. He didn't even say "Thanks."

"That's enough," I said when he was done with the Coke and the peanuts. "We can go out and play ball now."

"I want to see the rest," Bart said.

I was tired of showing him around. "There is no more," I told him. "Only Mom's office behind the registration desk. Storerooms and refrigerators in the basement. Boring stuff. Let's go out and play."

So we went outside. We threw the ball around for a little while. Dan, Bruce, and Gary were playing football out there, too. Acres of flat, grassy fields surrounded the Inn. There was plenty of room for all of us. We hadn't been playing for more than ten minutes, though, when Bart said, "I gotta go now. My mother'll be wondering what happened to me."

"But it's awful early," I said.

"Well, she doesn't know I'm here," he said.

"You could phone her," I said.

"Nah," he said. "She'll get mad. She likes me to come right home after school. But I'll come back another day. I'll tell her ahead of time and then she won't get mad."

"OK," I said. What else could I say? I watched him run all the way down the driveway. It wasn't until after I saw him cross the highway that I realized he'd taken my ball with him.

I went over to where Dan and the guys were playing. Naturally they didn't ask me to join them. Pretty soon I got tired of watching and went back in the building. I wandered into the bar again and sat down on a stool. As soon as he saw me, Tex started in. "The Lady Rosalie was playing in the garden," he said in a low, soft voice as he went right on polishing glasses. "She built little houses and people out of mud and sand. Then her friend, the fairy Rosamunde, touched them with her magic rose, and they all came alive, a whole living village of tiny farmers and housewives and carpenters and milkmaids." Tex stopped and looked at me, a smile in his eyes. It was my job to pick the story up at that point and continue it. We made up these fairy tales and told them to each other nearly every day. Sometimes the same one went on for months.

"I don't know what happened next," I said, "and I don't care. I'm tired of the Lady Rosalie and Count Blackrose and the whole court at Rosehilde. They're not real."

Poor Tex. He looked like he was going to faint. Just then, my mother came in the bar with Mr. Neumann, one of the liquor salesmen who called on her every week. I was relieved. Tex wouldn't say a word about the Land of Three Roses in front of them.

"Hi, Rosie. Hello, Tex," Mr. Neumann said.

"Hello, Rosie," my mother said. "How was school today?" I wanted to tell her about Millie's party, but I didn't get a chance. Right away she turned to Tex. "What do we need from Banner?" she asked him.

Banner was the firm Mr. Neumann worked for.

I hopped off the bar stool and stood near Mr. Neumann as he took his order pad out of his briefcase and put it up on the bar. "How're Harry and Bess?" I asked. Harry and Bess were Mr. Neumann's poodles. He had named them after the President, Harry Truman, and his wife.

"Rosie," Mom scolded, "don't bother Mr. Neumann while he's trying to write up an order."

"That's all right, Bea," Mr. Neumann said. "I can do two things at once."

"You better send us a case of Canadian Club," Tex said.

Mr. Neumann wrote that down while he answered me. "Harry and Bess are fine. Bess is pregnant. She's going to have a litter of pups any time now."

"Oh, Mr. Neumann, can I have one? Please, can I?" It was hopeless, but I wasn't going to let any chance pass me by.

"Rosie!" My mother was really annoyed with me now. "How many times have I told you—an inn is no place for a dog."

"I'm sorry, Rosie," Mr. Neumann said. "Anyway, I don't give my pups away. Toy poodles are too expensive for that. They cost so much to raise, I have to sell them to try to break even."

"Listen, Rosie," Mom said, "I promise, for your birthday, I'll get you a whole aquarium full of goldfish."

Did she really think a bunch of silent, cold-blooded fish swimming around in a tank was the same as a dog? A bunch of fish was no better than a picture on the wall or a philodendron plant. I already had eight different plants in my room that I'd bought with my own money. I didn't want any more decorations. I wanted a friend.

I decided to leave. As I was walking out, Mr. Neumann called to me, "When is your birthday anyway, Rosie?"

I stopped short and turned around. "December 16th," I said. "In a month and a half."

"An inn is no place for a dog," Mom repeated. "Messes in the lobby. Barking in the bedrooms. Let's not be ridiculous."

"But, Mom, I'd take perfect care of a dog. Nothing like that would happen. You're not being—"

My mother interrupted me. "We've been through this a dozen times. I don't want to hear another word about it. Not now. Not ever." I knew that tone of voice. There was nothing else to say, so I left.

I started up the stairs. I went very slowly. What could I do now, except my homework? Then I heard a faint yipping sound, far, far away. It was Buster. I remembered that I had promised Major Dunleigh I would walk Buster that afternoon. Between Millie's party and Bart's visit, I had forgotten.

I ran down the hall to room #17. I was really sorry I had been so fresh to Tex. Actually, I enjoyed the Land

28

of Three Roses as much as he did. After I'd walked Buster, I'd go to Tex and apologize.

I knocked on Mrs. Dunleigh's door. "Come in," she called so faintly in her thin, whispery voice that I could hardly hear her. "It's not locked." I pushed open the door. Mrs. Dunleigh was sitting up in her bed, wearing a pale gray bed jacket, the same color as most of her dresses, and as her hair too, which she always wore pulled off her face in a bun. Mom also had gray hair, but she bleached it, and went to the beauty parlor every week to have it set. No matter how busy she was, she always found time for that. During the war, when gas was rationed, she'd walked, even though it was almost two miles.

"I've come to take Buster out, Mrs. Dunleigh," I said. "The Major asked me to."

"Yes, dear," Mrs. Dunleigh replied softly. "That's so kind of you. You'll find your money on the bureau. I told the Major a quarter wasn't enough, so he left fifty cents."

"Oh, a quarter is plenty," I said. "I'm glad to do it. You know how much I like animals."

"Yes," Mrs. Dunleigh replied, "you're very kind." Buster was lying next to her, on top of the covers, and she picked him up. "Little Rosie loves you, honey-yunums," she said to Buster, holding him right in front of her face. "She loves you almost as much as Mommy does. She won't let any nasty automobiles run you over." She held him out to me. "His leash is in the night table drawer. You will be careful, won't you? It's gotten quite chilly out, hasn't it? Do you think we ought to put on his coat?"

I opened the drawer and got out the leash. "It's not really cold," I said. "There was a little wind while I was walking home from school, but I think it's died down now. Buster won't catch cold."

I put Buster down on the floor. I clipped the leash on his collar and led him out of the room. "Don't you think you'd better carry him?" Mrs. Dunleigh called after me as I shut the door. Her voice was very soft, even when she thought she was shouting, so I was able to pretend I didn't hear her.

Once we got outside, I went round to the back of the building where there was no danger of Mrs. Dunleigh's seeing me from her window. I had made up my mind. I was going to try to make a real dog out of Buster. He must have been a real dog once, before Mrs. Dunleigh got hold of him; maybe he could be one again.

I snapped the leash off Buster's collar and held it in my hand. I knew Buster wouldn't run away. He was too frightened to be by himself. Then I started to run— well, not run, exactly, but sort of trot. "Come on, Buster," I called. "Come on. Come with Rosie." Buster took two or three little hops in an effort to keep up with me. Really and truly, that dog was a good sport. But he had belonged to Mrs. Dunleigh too long, and he was old. He couldn't keep up, and he began to huff and puff with the effort. I certainly didn't want him dropping dead on me. Unlike Mom, Mrs. Dunleigh wasn't the type who lost her temper, but I knew she'd happily murder me if any harm came to Buster while he was in my care.

I picked him up and stroked his head for a few minutes. "Good doggie," I said. "Good little doggie. You tried. You did try. Next time I take you out, we'll try again. Maybe if you do a little each day, you'll build up your stamina." But of course I didn't know when I'd get another chance to walk Buster. Mrs. Dunleigh was always feeling ill, but this was the first time she'd felt so ill she was unable to walk Buster.

I put the leash back on the dog, put him on the ground, and walked with him slowly until he had done what he was supposed to do. Then I took him back to Mrs. Dunleigh.

"Did he make number two?" she asked me. Underneath the coats of white face powder she always wore, she blushed faintly.

"Yes," I said.

"Would you get me some toilet paper from the bathroom, please, Rosie, so I can wipe him?"

"Sure," I said. I tried hard not to smile. I went into the connecting bathroom and got some toilet paper and gave it to her.

"Take your money off the bureau, Rosie, dear," she said as she patted Buster's rear. "Take it all. You earned it."

31

So I took it. Luckily there was a wastebasket right by Mrs. Dunleigh's bed so she didn't ask me to dispose of the toilet paper. I put the money away in my room and then I went down to the bar. It was getting late. There probably would be customers in the bar, but I wanted to tell Tex I was sorry for the way I had acted. I wanted to tell him before it was too late.

There were six different people sitting at the bar when I got there, but they all had drinks in front of them. Four of the people were together, and the other two were a couple, so Tex didn't have to make conversation with any of them. I sat down on the very last stool, in the corner where the horseshoe-shaped bar met the wall. Tex came over to me. "What can I get you, Princess?" he asked. He didn't sound mad.

"I'm sorry I was fresh to you before," I said. "I didn't mean what I said about the Land of Three Roses. I love it; I really do."

"Oh, that's OK, Princess," Tex said. "I understand. You had other things on your mind. Maybe you're getting too old for fairy tales."

"No, I'm not," I said, "but I think I'm tired of the story we've been telling. It's not getting anywhere. It's just one magic trick after another, and the Lady Rosalie is just like the audience at the movies. She just sits there, watching. She doesn't *do* anything. If she gets into trouble, some prince or fairy always comes along and rescues her. That's boring."

"Well, let's start over," Tex said. "Let's start a new story."

"That's a good idea," I said. "You begin."

"OK," Tex said. "I'll think about it for a few minutes, while I check around and see if anyone wants another drink."

He thought, and I thought. When he returned, he started the story. "Back at time's beginning, in a far-away country, there lived a beautiful girl named Rosalie."

"She wasn't beautiful," I interrupted. "She was fat."

He stared at me thoughtfully for a moment. "OK," he said, "so she wasn't beautiful. But she wasn't bad. Although her face was covered with freckles, and her figure might be politely described as 'pleasingly plump,' she had thick, reddish-brown hair which she wore around her head in braids, and huge, midnight-blue eyes rimmed with long, heavy lashes." He stopped and looked at me again. "OK," he said. "Your turn."

"So soon?" I asked.

"Yes," he said. "I need some clues."

"Well," I informed him, "Rosalie lived all by herself in a tower. The door at the bottom of the tower steps was locked, and she could never go out. No one ever came in, either. Rosalie knew her name because there were signs in all the rooms in the tower: 'This is Rosalie's bed.' 'This is Rosalie's toothbrush.' 'This is Rosalie's diary.' And all the books had bookplates in them which read, 'Ex libris: Rosalie.' "

We went on like that for quite a while. It turned out to be a long story.

*B*ack at time's beginning, in a faraway country, there lived a young girl named Rosalie. She was not so beautiful as heroines are supposed to be, but she wasn't bad. Although her face was covered with freckles, and her figure might be politely described as pleasingly plump, she had thick, reddish-brown hair which she wore around her head in braids, and huge, midnight-blue eyes rimmed with long, heavy lashes.

Rosalie lived all by herself in a tower. The door at the bottom of the tower steps was locked, and she could never go out. No one ever came in, either. Rosalie knew her name because there were signs in all the rooms in the tower. "This is Rosalie's bed." "This is Rosalie's toothbrush." "This is Rosalie's diary." And all the books had bookplates in them which read, "Ex libris: Rosalie."

All of Rosalie's needs were supplied by magic. At mealtime perfectly cooked food appeared on the table. If she decided she was tired of eggs, she got no more eggs for weeks, until she decided she might like to try an egg again. She never had to express her thoughts out loud. As a matter of fact, she couldn't express them out loud, because she had never had any occasion to talk to anyone.

There were all kinds of toys and games in the tower, and like her clothes, they kept changing as she grew older. Music played much of the time, and the rooms were filled with pictures and statues. It was one of Rosalie's jobs to dust the pictures. She had other jobs too. She had her samplers to embroider, and her music lessons to practice. She was skillful on both the harpsichord and the viola, though of course, she could not sing a note.

There were no windows in the tower—only that locked and bolted door which Rosalie tried every morning and every evening, but which never yielded, no matter how hard she beat against it. For in spite of the fact that she couldn't see out of her tower, Rosalie knew that there was more to the world than what she saw. She knew that from her books, of which she had thousands, and which were full of all kinds of glorious pictures, in four or six or eight colors, of mountains and deserts, of toads and queens, of carts and elves, of planets and dandelions, of cities and buckets, of worms and bears. Rosalie liked the bears best.

Besides, every morning between nine and eleven, after she'd made her bed and dusted the pictures, a voice spoke to her. It was a soft, melodious voice and it told Rosalie all kinds of things.

It was the Voice which had taught her how to embroider samplers and play the harpsichord and viola. It was the Voice which soothed her on the very rare occasions when she was ill. Rosalie did not get sick very often because there was no one from whom to catch any diseases, but once in a while some germ did sneak in through an invisible crack in the wall, and she got a stuffed nose or sore throat. The Voice also tried to comfort her when she'd had a nightmare, but that wasn't much use, since the Voice spoke to her only between nine and eleven, several hours after both the bad dream and the long black shadows in her head had entirely disappeared.

The Voice told Rosalie when it was her birthday, and played a treasure hunt game with her, leading her to look for secret gifts underneath the bed, in back of the cupboard, or behind the bottles of cod liver oil and jars of cold cream in the medicine cabinet. The presents were always wonderful things, like a conch shell in which Rosalie could hear the ocean, a whale's tooth on a chain to wear around her neck, a painted Easter egg with a glass window at one end through which Rosalie could see a whole little village, or a seed rock which when dropped in water sprouted fairy worlds of crystal caves and caverns. Of course, by the time Rosalie's eleventh birthday came around, she didn't need any voice to tell her what day it was. She had learned perfectly well how to keep track of the days for herself. She had a clock to tell her the time and it was another one of her tasks to wind it every night, which she did with perfect faithfulness because she was very worried, in her windowless world, at the idea of its stopping. If it stopped, she would have no idea of when to lie down or when to get up or when her birthday was coming.

She was so excited the morning of her eleventh birthday that she woke up at six, a whole hour early, with a strange feeling in the pit of her stomach, an odd mixture of fear and anticipation such as she had never felt before. The anticipation she recognized; she always felt it as her birthday approached. Her birthday was extremely important to her because, after all, nothing else ever happened in her world. There were never any surprises or excitement, not so much as a clap of thunder or an unexpected fly walking across the kitchen ceiling. But fear was something she had never felt before, and the only reason she was able to identify it as part of her feelings on the morning of her eleventh birthday was because she had read vivid descriptions of it in some of her books.

It was so early that her breakfast wasn't even ready. She dressed in her loveliest gown, a green plaid taffeta that had shown up in her wardrobe

only the day before yesterday. Then she went down to the music room to practice her instruments. She found it difficult to concentrate on the lessons, but she forced her mind to stick to its business because she had to do something to occupy herself until breakfast at seven, clean-up at eight, and the visit of her Voice at nine. Even so, she was done with everything by quarter of nine, and the last fifteen minutes she spent in the great hall, sitting on her old wicker rocking chair that she had carried down from her bedroom, with her favorite dilapidated doll in her lap, watching the clock.

No sooner had the last echo of the clock bird's ninth "cuckoo" died out than she heard the Voice speak to her. "Happy birthday, dear Rosalie," it said in its even, melodic tones. "What a lovely day for your birthday."

"Is it?" Rosalie replied—not out loud, of course, but the Voice never had any trouble responding to her thoughts. "I wouldn't know. I'm not allowed out."

"I know that, dear Rosalie," said the Voice. "That's for your own good."

"Perhaps I ought to be the judge of that," Rosalie replied crossly.

"What's the matter with you today?" asked the Voice, as evenly and melodically as ever. "Don't you feel well?"

"I know what I want for my birthday," Rosalie replied. "I want to go outside. Or at least see outside. That's what I want. I'm sick and tired of magic eggs and whales' teeth. I want to see what the real world is like for once."

"Rosalie, what's come over you?" The Voice actually sounded a tiny bit disturbed. "I've never heard you talk like this before."

"You don't see me every morning when I first get up and every night right before I go to bed. You don't see me beating and banging at that door," Rosalie said.

"How long has that been going on?" the Voice asked. "How come no one told me of this?"

"Who's to tell you?" Rosalie reminded the Voice. "No one any smarter than a germ has ever been inside this place, except for you and me. Whoever it is that brings my food and mops the kitchen floor—they don't know anything. They're just invisible hands. They don't have minds, or anything like that."

"How do you know, Rosalie?" the Voice asked.

"If there were another mind around here, don't you think I'd feel it? If there were even as much of a mind as a puppy has, I'd know. Wait!" she exclaimed suddenly. "I have an idea. How about giving me a dog or a cat? Or even a bird or a goldfish."

"Oh, dear Rosalie," the Voice said sadly, "dear,

dear Rosalie, what makes you think I could let you out even if I wanted to? Or let anything else in, for that matter."

"Well, if you can't," Rosalie cried silently, "who can? Who can? It wasn't meant to be this way. I'm sure of that. It's not natural."

"Don't you want to play our game?" the Voice queried hopefully. Rosalie knew she was being diverted. "Don't you want to see what you got for your birthday?"

"If it isn't an open window or an open door, no," Rosalie replied stubbornly, "no, I don't want to see it."

"So you're just going to sit there all day, like a mule?" the Voice inquired in a tone of sweet reason. "What's the good of that?"

"I'm going to sit here like a mule," Rosalie said, "until you do something for me that's of some use to me."

"Why, Rosalie," the Voice said, "you hurt me to the quick. Haven't I done everything of use for you—everything? I've taught you to read and write. I've taught you to play the harpsichord and the viola. I've taught you to sew and to knit, to embroider and to crochet. Next week I was going to start cooking lessons. But if you're going to behave so childishly, I won't do it. Little children can't be trusted near hot stoves."

"I'd like to learn to cook," Rosalie replied, "but I don't want to learn to cook badly enough to wait around here another whole year. I spend my time doing what you want me to do. I was usually glad enough for that, because how would I have filled the hours if it weren't for the things you've taught me? But today's my birthday. You want me to go on that treasure hunt. You like it each time I get excited about one of the things you've picked out for me. Well, if you want me to look for presents, you'll have to do what I want, for once."

"Rosalie, I said it before, and I'll say it again." The Voice sounded somewhat exasperated. "What makes you think I can let you out?"

"I believe you can," Rosalie insisted. "I think you just don't want to. But let that go for a minute. Let's pretend that you can't let me out. Certainly you can answer some questions for me."

"Well, Rosalie, I'll try. I have always tried to answer your questions. You know that."

"Never before have I asked the right ones," Rosalie said. "For example, who am I?"

"That *is* a silly question," the Voice responded. "You know who you are. You're Rosalie."

"Who is she?" Rosalie asked desperately. "Who's her mother? Who's her father? Why is she locked up in a windowless tower? Who is it

41

that sends her books and food? And who are you? Next to who I am, that's what I want to know most of all. Who are you?"

"Whoa, there, Rosalie," the Voice cried. "That's too many questions. I can't answer them all at once."

"You don't have to answer them all at once," Rosalie said. "One at a time will do perfectly well."

"I can't answer your questions," the Voice said. "I can't answer any of them. That would be dangerous. But I can tell you this much," the Voice went on slowly. "Be glad you're in here. The world outside is a dangerous place. If you put one foot outside the tower door, your safe, comfortable life will be over. I don't think you'd last out there for a day and a half. You'd be dead long before you'd found the answers to any of your foolish questions."

"Is that what you think?" Rosalie asked. "You don't think very much of me at all, then, do you? After all these years, you don't think I can do anything."

"Rosalie," the Voice returned sharply, "listen to me. When I say the world outside is dangerous, I know what I'm talking about. Your tower is located in a section of the Land of Three Roses called County Blackrose. The King of this land, though kind enough, is also weak and foolish. He

42

has not been able to prevent his younger brother and heir, Count Blackrose, from becoming an absolute tyrant. It is Count Blackrose who rules in this district, not the King from his court in the capital city of Rosehilde. If you stepped out of your tower door, you would be in his power, and how he hates little girls with roses in their names and freckles on their faces. Who knows what he would do to you? I tremble to think of it. That's why I want you to stay here, inside, where no harm will come to you."

"Isn't that for me to decide?" Rosalie said. "It's my life, after all."

"Don't be so sure of that," the Voice said. "People often have to do things they don't want to do."

"But at least they know why," Rosalie said. "How can I agree that it's best for me to stay locked up in here if I don't know why?"

"I've told you why. It's dangerous out there."

"That's not a good enough reason."

"Rosalie, Rosalie, accept what I say," the Voice begged softly, in the soothing tones it had used when hot milk and honey had appeared on Rosalie's night table the time she stayed in bed all day because her throat was sore. "I know best, indeed I do. Things are the way they have to be."

Rosalie shut her mind away from the Voice and would communicate with it no longer. She sat in her chair stony-faced for a long time, and though she could sense that the Voice was still with her in the room, she would have nothing to do with it.

At last the Voice spoke again. "Rosalie," it said, "my time is almost up. You know that. Soon I must go. Won't you go look for your presents before I leave? Won't you do that one little thing for me, your old friend? Please, Rosalie. In memory of all that we've done together."

So Rosalie got up off her chair. "Very well," she said. She didn't say it graciously, but at least she said it. She followed the Voice down, down, down the winding steps that ran from the top of the tower to the bottom, and then down, down, through a trapdoor, into the dirt-floored dungeons that lay beneath. Rosalie had never been so deep before. It was pitch black, except for the dim light cast by the candle that the Voice had told Rosalie to take from the kitchen. Once again, Rosalie felt fear grip her stomach, but she said nothing about it to the Voice and pushed on through cavernous rooms she'd never before known existed. And then, suddenly, there in the middle of the biggest room of all, she came upon the gift. It was a pot, and growing in the pot was a gardenia plant, with dark shiny leaves and huge white flowers whose thick, sweet scent overcame the dank odors that

44

hung in the damp underground air. Rosalie gasped with pleasure when she saw it. She had not meant to give the Voice the satisfaction of hearing or seeing her enjoy any of the gifts, but she couldn't help it. If she could not have an animal, at least, it seemed, she could have a plant. She picked it up in her arms and said, "Thank you, thank you. It's very lovely."

"You're welcome," the Voice said, a little smugly. And then the Voice led her upstairs again, up, up, up to the little tiny room at the very top of the tower, and there Rosalie found an amazing doll house with eighteen rooms completely furnished, down to the plates in the cupboard, the chamber pots in the bedrooms, and little boxes of snuff on the drawing room tables. Ten dolls lived in it—a husband, a wife, three children, and six servants. A dog, a cat, and a bird lived there too. With that doll house, a person could almost make a world. Almost. The Voice was trying. Rosalie knew it. "Thank you," she said again. "Thank you very much."

And then the Voice led her into her own bedroom and told her to open the top drawer of her bureau, and there Rosalie found a flat box wrapped in gold paper and tied with a gold ribbon. Slowly, carefully, Rosalie undid the ribbon and the paper, very slowly, very carefully. She had her own ways of teasing the Voice, and had used them for years. At last the package was unwrapped, the lid of the box was removed, and the gift, lying on white cotton, was revealed. When that moment came, the Voice uttered a hoarse scream. "We are lost! We are lost!" it cried. As Rosalie gazed down into the box, she knew why the Voice had screamed.

For on the cotton, sparkling and shining in the clear white light that filled the tower day and night, lay a key, a great golden key. Rosalie knew, without being told, which door that key would open.

"Throw it away, Rosalie," the Voice said in a horrified whisper. "Take that key downstairs and throw it in the garbage pail in the kitchen."

"No," Rosalie replied with perfect firmness.

"The hands will come and take it away from you," the Voice threatened.

"It's not their time," Rosalie replied. "When they come again, I shall be long gone!"

The Voice sighed, a huge sigh of defeat. "All right," she said. "All right, Old One. All right, Blackrose. All right, Liederkranz. All right, whichever one of you it was that did this thing. Whatever happens now is on your head." And then the Voice was gone. As always, Rosalie could tell the very moment that it was no longer there.

She picked the key up and held it in her hand, bewitched for a moment by its golden splendor. Then she ran as quickly as she could down the long, winding tower steps.

R my name is Rosie,
And my husband's name is Ralph,
And we come from Rhode Island,
And we sell Roses.

After that I went on to "S my name is Susie," "T my name is Tina," "U my name is Una," and "V my name is Vickie," before I missed. I was playing ball in the school yard with the other girls. Playing alone was no good. It didn't matter if you got all the way to "Z my name is Zelda." If you were alone, who knew?

Millie Van Dyke was absent anyway. Maybe she'd eaten too much ice cream at her birthday party and gotten a stomach ache. Maybe she had appendicitis and was in the hospital. Maybe she wouldn't come back to school for six months. Maybe she'd never come back at all. Maybe she was dead.

"You shoulda' been there," Cheryl said. "It was a terrific party. We each got a set of jacks with two balls and a jump rope. Each jump rope had different colored handles. You shoulda' been there."

"I would have been there," I said very slowly and distinctly, "if I had been invited."

"Oh, dear," Cheryl said. "I didn't know. I thought your mother wouldn't let you come or something. I'm sorry." She turned to Estelle Coviella. "Wasn't it funny, though, when Carl came in without saying a word and ate three pieces of cake? Wasn't it funny?"

"It doesn't sound funny to me," I said. "Carl is a pig."

"I'm tired of talking about that old party," Estelle said. "Let's talk about something else. You'd think it was the only thing that had ever happened around here. Rosie, you want to come over my house after school? We can make up stories with my new Betty Grable paper dolls."

"I can't," I replied. "It's dark by 4:30. My mother won't let me cross the highway after dark. During the winter, I have to go right home after school."

"Don't you know that, Estelle?" Cheryl said. Estelle was new that year. "Even though she works, Rosie's mother takes good care of her, just like other people's mothers."

I ignored Cheryl. She was a rat, and everyone knew

it. "I can come over Saturday, if you want," I said to Estelle.

"I'm going to Plainfield, to my grandmother's, for the weekend," Estelle replied apologetically. "To see my old friends from before I moved."

"Maybe another Saturday," I said.

Estelle nodded. "Another Saturday. I'll let you know."

The bell rang and we went back into the building. Afterwards, when school let out, Bart walked with me again. He caught up with me after I'd gone halfway. He wasn't actually going to let anyone *see* him walking with me. But that was OK. I wasn't too crazy to have anyone see me walking with him either. He wasn't exactly number one in Miss Chardip's fifth grade.

"I can stay longer today," Bart said. "I can stay for dinner."

"You'll have to come for dinner some other time," I told him. "Tonight I have to work."

"You have to work?" Bart asked. He was amazed. "Fifth graders can't work. It's against the law or something."

"They can help their mothers," I said. "That's not against the law. You help your mother, don't you?"

"Yeah," Bart said. "I didn't think it was the same thing. What do you do?"

"There's a banquet tonight. When the dinners are dished up, Luke, the chef, puts the turkey on the plate, and Pedro puts on the mashed potatoes. Mom puts on the peas, Rachel puts on the gravy, and I put on the parsley."

"What about your brother Dan? What does he do?"

"He listens to the radio. He hates to help."

"But you like to?" Bart asked.

"Not really," I admitted. "Putting on parsley is a dumb job. I wish I could put on the peas or the gravy. That'd be more interesting."

When we got home, we went right into the kitchen. Min was hurrying back and forth between the kitchen and the Holiday Room carrying racks of glasses and silverware and piles of plates. Tex was pouring himself a cup of coffee from the urn. Sylvester, the porter, was scrubbing pots because the dishwasher hadn't shown up for the second time that week. Luke was slicing a thirty-pound turkey. It looked big as an eagle. He arranged layers of dark and light meat on top of squares of stuffing placed in rows on large, flat baking pans. Other turkeys were lined up, waiting their turn. Their skins were all brown and crisp, and their fat legs were sticking up in the air.

"Hey, Luke," I said, "don't you think I'm ready for a promotion? Don't you think I could go up to gravy or peas tonight? I'm old enough."

"The gravy is awful hot, honey," Luke said. "What if you spill it? And the peas are hard to handle. If you don't put 'em on the plate just so, they slide all over and get mixed up with the gravy."

51

"Everyone around here thinks I'm a baby," I protested. "Well, I'm not. I'm a lot handier than Rachel. I can knit and embroider and crochet, and she can't do any of those things. I'm a lot less likely to spill the gravy than she is."

"I'll take a piece of turkey," Bart said.

Luke handed over a slice of white meat. "I like dark meat better," Bart said. "You can give me a couple of slices on a plate, with some of that stuffing."

"It's cold," Luke said.

"Well, maybe you could heat it up in the oven," Bart suggested. "Give me some potatoes and cranberry sauce too." So Luke put a portion of turkey—all dark meat—on a pie tin, poured some gravy over it, and heated it in the oven for a few minutes. "The mashed potatoes aren't ready yet," he said. "Will you settle for some french fries?"

Bart said that'd be all right. Luke fried some up for him in the deep fat. Pedro dished him a monster portion of pie and ice cream, which I carried into the Holiday Room, because his hands were full with the turkey platter and a plate of rolls and butter. I watched him eat every bit of that food. Between bites, he didn't even bother to shut his mouth. He had gotten his dinner after all. Min and two other waitresses who only worked parties were busy all around us setting up for the Lions Club Ladies' Night banquet which would begin in a few hours.

After Bart had eaten all the food, he said, "I'm

thirsty. Let's get a Coke." I followed him into the bar. By now he knew the way.

Tex wasn't there. Maybe he was still drinking coffee in the kitchen, or maybe he was downstairs, tapping a keg of beer or filling a carton with the liquor he needed for the night's business. I went behind the bar and drew Bart a Coke from the tap. I put it up in front of Bart, and then I drew one for myself too.

"Is there money in the cash register?" Bart asked.

"I guess so," I said.

"So long as you're back there, why don't you open it up and find out? I could use a couple of bucks' worth of quarters."

"Are you crazy?" I laughed. I thought he was joking.

He wasn't. "It's your cash register, isn't it?" he asked. "Can't you take whatever you want out of it?"

"No, Bart Flint, I cannot, any more than I can eat all the ice cream I want."

"Oh, sure you can," he urged. "Who'll know it was you? They'll think it was that crummy bartender, with the long, gloomy face. Come on, Rosie, don't be a piker." He smiled at me. I didn't smile back. For a while I had thought he looked a little bit like Van Johnson. Now I thought he looked like a weasel.

I grabbed the glass of Coke that I had put in front of him, spilled it out into the bar sink, and threw the ice in after it. "OK, Bart," I said, "get out of here. Go on home."

The smile was wiped right off his face. "Hey," he

whined, "what's the big idea? What'd ya do that for?"

"Never mind," I said. "Just get out of here."

"Suppose I don't want to?" he asked. His voice sounded like I'd hurt him, instead of the other way round.

"If you don't leave," I replied between my teeth, "I will find my mother. I will tell her you wanted me to steal from the cash register for you. That's what I'll tell her."

"Is it stealing if you take your own money?" He wasn't crazy; he was just dumb. He didn't understand anything at all about how a business is run.

"It's not my money," I answered. "If I take it, I am stealing. You have the wrong idea about this place, Bart, and you have the wrong idea about me. Now, get out of here."

Bart seemed very surprised. He could not have been more surprised at me, though, than I was at him. But I should have guessed. He'd scattered lots of clues. He opened his mouth as if he were going to say something else, but then he decided against it. He shut his mouth, got off the bar stool, and walked out of the bar. That was the end of that. Some friend. I was too angry to even cry.

I went to find my mother. She was in her private office, behind the registration desk, balancing cash.

"Hey, Mom," I said, "you know what that rat Bart wanted me to do?"

My mother was in the middle of counting a pile of

dollar bills and she waved her hand at me to be quiet. "Now look what you've done," she said. "You've made me lose count. I'll have to start all over again."

I felt my throat grow tight. I knew that in a minute the tears would start to come. When she finally looked up at me, Mom knew it too. "Oh, for heaven's sake, Rosie, don't start that again," she scolded. "Here, count the quarters. Put them into ten-dollar piles so I can wrap them."

I pulled a chair up to her big desk and sat down opposite her. I counted out the quarters, the dimes, and the pennies. When I was finished, I said to her, "Now can I tell you what happened?"

"Tell me at supper, Rosie," she said, pushing herself away from the desk. "I have to get into the kitchen and see if Luke's ready for tonight." But I knew there'd be no chance to talk to her when we three ate. With a banquet tonight, she'd never be able to sit down with us.

I followed her out of the office. "Listen, Mom," I said very fast. "That Bart is a louse. He wanted me to take money out of the cash register and give it to him."

But she wasn't really listening. "Is that so?" she said as she went right on walking.

"I won't let him come over again. I thought he was going to be a friend."

"Invite another friend over," Mom said, "not Bart, whoever he is. I don't think I know him, do I?"

"I don't have any other friends," I said.

"Of course you have other friends," Mom insisted. She pushed open the swinging door into the kitchen.

"Who?" I asked. "Name one, one real friend."

But she was already talking to Luke and Minnie. "There'll be seventy-three tonight," she said, "eight more than they guaranteed originally. I'll tell Sylvester to bring in a small round. That'll be better than trying to squeeze extra places at the tables you've already set."

I tugged at her sleeve, like a three-year-old. "Mom," I said, "Mom, don't you understand? He wanted me to take money out of the cash register!"

She turned and looked at me for one second. "That's terrible, honey," she said. Then she went back to her conversation with Luke and Minnie. "Two people are on special diets and have to eat broiled fish. Minnie, the chairman will point them out to you. Do we have any fresh sole, Luke?"

I ran out of the kitchen and up to my room. I was sure no one even noticed that I had gone. I lay down on my bed and started to cry. I cried as loud as I could. Maybe they'd hear me sobbing all the way downstairs.

I wished I was dead. If I were dead, Mom would feel terrible. Then she would notice I was gone, all right. She'd feel sick about the times she'd ignored me. She'd hate herself for having scolded me. She scolded me for whining. She scolded me for bothering her when she was busy. She scolded me for leaving my room messy. She scolded me for not feeling well and staying home from school, as if I could help it when I didn't feel well. If I were dead, she'd be sorry for all that.

But it wasn't Mom who heard me crying. It was Rachel. "Wash up," she said as she came into my room without knocking. "Come down and have some supper."

"I don't want any supper," I said. "I just want to die. I think I'll kill myelf."

"Why would you want to do that?" Rachel asked. She didn't sound upset, but she did sound as if she really wanted to know. She sat down on the edge of my bed and looked at me.

I sat up to explain. "Oh, Bart turned out to be a rat," I told her. "He wanted me to take money out of the cash register and give it to him."

"If that's the case," Rachel said, "he's certainly not worth killing yourself over."

That sounded reasonable, so I told her the rest. "No one loves me, Rachel," I said. I wasn't even crying anymore. I felt as if I were just speaking the simple truth.

"That's ridiculous," Rachel said. I knew she'd say that. Really, she was no help. "You have more friends around this place than anyone else," she went on.

"I'm not talking about them. I'm talking about my family."

"You think Mother doesn't love you?" Rachel asked. "That's the most ridiculous thing of all."

"Maybe it is," I said, "but she certainly doesn't *act* as if she loves me. I think she's forgotten. She never really hears what I say. But if I were dead, she'd know she'd loved me all right. Boy, would she feel sick about all the times she'd ignored me!"

"People have the wrong idea about being dead," Rachel said. "People who commit suicide really believe in their hearts that they're going to be watching everyone else weeping and crying and feeling guilty at the funeral. I mean, we all know that dead people don't realize what's going on. We know it in our heads, but people who kill themselves don't really believe it. Not in their hearts, they don't. But they're wrong. When you're dead, you're dead, and you don't get to see all the people you're mad at feeling miserable. So what's the use of dying? It's pointless really." She actually smiled. "You wouldn't like it at all. So instead of killing yourself, come down and have some supper."

"It's not funny," I told her. "It's not funny one little bit."

She nodded. "I know that, Rosebud, but I still think that if you had some supper, you'd feel better."

"Not now," I said. "Maybe later. You go ahead."

"OK," Rachel said. "I can't wait. I'm starved."

So she left. I lay on my bed for a while longer. Maybe I fell asleep for a few minutes. Later I heard the deep rumble of mingled voices coming up through the floor. That's how I knew the lobby was full of people.

58

I got off my bed and went out into the hall. The noise of people was much louder and clearer now. At the top of the stairs, I lay down on my belly, with my elbows on the floor and my head held up in my hands. In that position, I had a perfect view of the lobby. I could see everything that was going on. When Dan and I were smaller, we used to lie like that all the time, watching. We'd count the fur coats, we'd laugh at the silly hats, we'd make fresh remarks about people who acted dumb. If Mom ever happened to look up as she walked across the lobby, she'd notice us and run upstairs quickly to send us to bed. But most times she didn't look up. We'd just stay there until we got bored or sleepy. Sometimes we stayed up till midnight and she never knew.

But Dan had gotten too old for such entertainment. It had been months since he had watched with me. It wasn't much fun alone, so I rarely did it nowadays myself. The people I was watching from the Lions Club were a dull-looking bunch anyway. Soon Rachel would be coming after me to put on the parsley. Well, I wouldn't do it. Let the waitresses put on their own crummy parsley.

I saw Mom come out of the bar and walk across the lobby, dodging the people who were crowding the room. She was banging a set of four chimes with a little mallet. "Dinner is served," she announced. "Dinner is served. Please go into the Holiday Room. Dinner is served."

I felt pretty hungry myself. I hadn't had any supper, after all. "Mom—ee, Mom—ee," I shouted at the top of my lungs. I surprised myself as that cry came out of my mouth. I wondered what I was doing. It could only, as Mom herself would have said, end in tears.

Mom looked up, saw me, and came dashing up the stairs. "My God, Rosie," she said, "what's the matter with you? What are you screaming for?"

"I'm hungry," I said. "I'm tired. How can I sleep with all this noise around here?"

Mom was very angry, of course. I knew she would be, but I wasn't really sorry. "Rosie, what's gotten into you?" she asked sharply. "You've gone crazy. Now just shut up. Go back to your room and shut up. I never heard of anyone screaming like that. The whole lobby full of customers could hear you."

I began to cry. "Let them hear me," I sobbed. "So what? I don't care."

"Well, I do," Mom said. "Now stop your everlasting whining and weeping and get yourself out of here, before I give you something to really cry about." I knew she would hit me, too, because she was mad enough. I picked myself up and limped back to my room, sobbing all the way.

A few minutes later, there was a knock on the door. Was it Mom, come back to apologize? I ran to open it, but it wasn't Mom. It was Tex. I must have been awfully loud if he'd heard me, too, in the bar. "Come on downstairs," he said. "It's time to dish up the dinners. Luke needs you."

"I'm not coming," I said. "I'm sick of parsley. I never want to see another piece of parsley as long as I live." I plopped down angrily on my bed.

"Luke said to tell you he's promoting you. He said to tell you tonight you move up to the gravy."

At first I didn't really believe Tex. "This afternoon Luke said I couldn't do the gravy. You heard him. He said I was too young."

Tex shrugged. "Well, he changed his mind. A person is entitled to change his mind."

I wanted to put the gravy on the turkey because it was a real job. The parsley was just make-work. The waitresses used to do it themselves, as they put the plates on their trays. It hadn't taken them any time at all. The gravy was different. They couldn't do that after the plates were on the trays. Someone had to stand on the line to do that.

So I washed my face at the sink in the corner of my room and went downstairs. Tex was too busy to wait for me, and he had left as soon as he saw me get off my bed. I went into the kitchen, took a white apron out of Luke's drawer, tied it around me, and went behind the steam table. Luke had taken the first tray of turkey portions out of the oven. He was beginning to lay the meat out on plates. Pedro was ready to dish up the mashed potatoes. Rachel held a slotted spoon in her hand for the peas. I took the dipper out of the gravy pot, which was sunk into the steam table. I would take the plates from Rachel, put gravy on the turkey and potatoes, and then place the plates on the wooden table to my right. There the waitresses would pick them up and arrange them on their trays.

My mother came in to give the signal to start dishing up. She too reached into Luke's drawer in front of the wooden table for a white apron. Usually the peas were her job. But then she saw that four of us were behind the steam table. She saw me there too, instead of in front, next to the parsley bowl.

Before Mom could open her mouth, Luke said, "Well, Mrs. Gold, you really ought to be out with the banquet where they need you. You shouldn't be back here, dishing up. Rachel can do the peas, and Rosie can do the gravy, and the girls can put on their own parsley. It'll be just as fast that way, and you won't be wasting your time back here."

I looked at my mother, wondering what she was going to say. Less than half an hour ago, she had been furious with me. I had been nothing to her but a big baby.

She glanced at me, and then turned back to Luke. Her face was serious, but it was no longer angry. "OK, Luke," she said. "You're right. With a dining room full of customers, I belong out there, not in here." She put the apron back in the drawer and went out through the swinging doors.

Very carefully I poured a dipperful of gravy on each portion of turkey. I hardly got the gravy mixed up with the peas at all. Afterwards, Luke made up an extra turkey dinner for me. I ate it sitting at the end of the bar with Tex, who was grabbing a bite too, before the banquet was over and all the Lions and Lionesses came back for another drink. We told each other our story.

Rosalie clutched the key tightly in her hand as she ran down the stairs. For all she knew, it might disappear as suddenly as it had come. It was surprisingly heavy, as heavy as if it were made out of lead instead of gold. Perhaps, she thought, it really isn't gold at all, only gold plated over some baser metal. But who cared? All that mattered was that it fit the lock.

At the foot of the stairs she came to the door. She placed the key in the lock. It fit perfectly, and turned the lock as easily as if it had been used every day.

Rosalie pushed open the door. It too responded immediately to her touch. She pushed much harder than necessary and found herself virtually hurtled through the doorway and out onto the green grass that lay beyond. She heard the door swing shut behind her, and she turned immediately to try it again. It was locked as tight as ever, and the key was still in the lock on the inside. She couldn't get back into the tower, even if she wanted to, and here she was on the outside, with no clothes except the green plaid gown she was wearing, nothing to eat, and not even an umbrella to keep her dry in case it rained. Among all the multitudes of pictures in her books, there had been no picture of an umbrella. It is, after all, impossible for even a thousand books to have pictures in them of everything.

Rosalie stood for a moment staring at her high stone tower. She shivered briefly as a cool breeze hit her shoulders, and she felt the clench of fear in her stomach that she had experienced that morning when she had first awakened. Now she knew why.

But the breeze died, and the warmth of the sun enveloped her like a blanket. She turned away from the tower and looked down the smooth expanse of green lawn that stretched before her. Above, the sky was blue and cloudless, and here and there on the lawn, bright dandelions grew like stars in the grass. The Voice had been right. It was a fine day for her eleventh birthday.

She started to walk across the grass. She wanted to find out what lay beyond the line of trees that stretched along the horizon. It was quite a long walk, actually, to the grove of trees, longer than she had thought at first, and the farther she walked, the less smooth and manicured was the grass. The ground became stubby and stony, and she realized she was on a lawn no longer, but in an untended field where nothing grew except clumps of wild onion. She stumbled on the rocks a couple of times, and once she even fell, tore her dress, and scraped her knee. As she picked herself up, she turned and looked back over the way she had come. She could no longer see the tower, even though the grove on the horizon seemed as far away as it had when she had started out.

But she reached it at last. The shade was welcome because it had grown unpleasantly warm as she had crossed the field. The temperature in the tower had always been exactly 72 degrees Fahrenheit, winter and summer, day and night. Rosalie was sweating for the first time in her life.

She sat down under the spreading branches of a pin oak tree to rest. She began to wonder what exactly was going to happen to her now. She had a curious feeling about herself, as if she were a character in one of her books. She seemed to be watching herself in this strange and mystifying situation from a remote distance, as if a window had suddenly appeared in the topmost room of her tower, and she were still there, looking at this odd, straggly girl stumbling and stubbing her way across the field to a brief refuge beneath a pin oak tree.

She didn't sit still long. She knew she had to find her way to food and shelter before dark. Her experience that morning in the tower cellars had taught her that dark was something she wouldn't care to be out in. She picked her way through the grove. It was difficult going because the roots of trees humped up through the dirt, and she had to bend almost to the ground to escape low-hanging branches that seemed to be reaching for her face. It was at one of those moments when she was bent almost double that she suddenly found herself sliding, sliding down a slippery mud bank and landing with fierce and unexpected speed in icy-cold water.

Rosalie had no more idea than a cat of how to swim, and she felt herself hurled along by the swift current of the stream. She struggled desperately to keep her head out of water, but twice the current forced her under, and the third time, she knew, would be the last time. She had read about that too in her books. But before the third time came, the stream had carried her into a calm, still pool, in the middle of which floated a rowboat. In the rowboat sat an old man, fishing.

He reached out an oar. Rosalie grabbed it, and he pulled her into his boat.

"It took you long enough to get here," he said, as she sat there shivering and gasping for breath. "I've been waiting all day."

He was the first living human being Rosalie had ever laid eyes on, at least within her memory. She had always thought she must have seen at least her mother, however briefly, at the moment she was born, and perhaps longer, for someone must have nursed her and changed her diapers in the time before her memory had begun. But this man was the first person she could be sure was really there. She had never spoken aloud, and she was unable to begin now. She just sat there, staring in dumb amazement, her teeth chattering wildly, and her plaid gown plastered to her skin like fish scales.

"Here," the old man said, "wrap yourself in this." He tossed her a thick sheepskin jacket that had been lying in the bottom of the boat. She put it on and in a few minutes she felt the warmth returning to her bones. The old man pulled in his fishing lines, picked up the oars, and began to row toward the shore of the pool, where weeping willows drooped over the bank. "What kept you?" he asked again. "Do you think I've nothing to do all day but sit here in the middle of the pool pretending to fish? There's nothing to catch here anyway. The Old One cleaned it all out long ago."

"I didn't know you were expecting me." Rosalie managed to get her voice going at last. It grated a little, like a rusty hinge, but she found she got the hang of using it rather quickly. "I didn't know where I was going, and I fell into the river, and I almost drowned."

"River?" the old man asked derisively. "What river? Do you call this little old stream a river? You can walk across the stones in most places and never even get your ankles wet. This pool is the deepest place."

"It's got a current swift as the wind," Rosalie said. "It swept me along at such a rate I was sure I would drown."

"It has scarcely more current than this pool," the old man insisted. "Don't make up silly stories to explain why you took a swim instead of coming by the bridge. I told the missus, I told her this very morning, her idea of taking in a charity case to do the heavy work was stupid. There isn't one of 'em, I said, who can be trusted. They're all lazy and they're all dumb. See how right I was? Here you are, taking a swim, ruining the only dress you've got, so we'll have to give you a new one, and you haven't done one stick of work yet, not one stick of work."

"Are you sure I'm the charity case you're expecting?" Rosalie asked hesitantly.

"Fat with freckles?" the old man snorted. "I guess you are. One good thing, anyway, it won't hurt you to lose a bit of weight."

By this time they had reached the shore. The old man hopped out of the boat and held it while Rosalie climbed out. He did not offer to help her, and as soon as her feet touched dry land, he said to her, "Beach the boat. Put it up on those sawhorses over there." Then he turned his back on her and began to walk up a path.

"And then what, sir?" she called out. "Then what should I do?" He was the most unpleasant person she could imagine, bald as a button, with long white hairs growing out of his squashed, wide nostrils, but she feared that if he disappeared entirely, she would never find a place to dry off or a bit of bread to assuage the hunger pains that were attacking her fiercely now.

"Follow the path," he called back without even bothering to turn around. "It'll take you up to the house. Be careful no harm comes to my jacket. If it does, you'll have to make it up out of your wages."

She tossed the jacket on the bank and then pulled the boat up on the shore. It was heavy, but she managed at last to stow it upside-down on the two sawhorses beneath one of the willows

69

that hung over the water's edge, and then, putting the jacket back on, she climbed up the steep, sandy path.

After a few moments she came into a dirt clearing filled with squawking chickens and ducks and a great deal of dung. In the middle was a cottage made out of clay with a thatched roof. It was badly in need of whitewashing, it had no windows, and weeds were growing in the thatch. The door, hanging on one hinge, was ajar, and a scrawny woman with scraggly iron-gray hair and a nose like a pelican's beak stood in the doorway. "So, you've come at last," she said. "Took you long enough to stow the boat. What were you doing down there anyway? Picking posies? Get inside and get out of that wet dress before you catch pneumonia. That's all I need, a charity girl who's too sick to work. I told Mr. Limberger, I told him this idea of his to get a charity case to do the heavy work was the stupidest idea he'd ever had. And since he's had nothing but stupid ideas since the day we were married, that's saying quite a good deal. What's your name, girl?" she added as she stood aside to let Rosalie pass into the dark, foul-smelling cottage.

"Rosalie," she replied somewhat hesitantly. Here in this cottage, the name Rosalie seemed somehow absurd.

"Rosalie. Hah!" the old woman exclaimed derisively. "What kind of name is that for a poor girl who has to earn her own living?"

"You could call me Rosie, ma'am," Rosalie suggested.

"Rosie? Rosie?" The old woman laughed out loud. "Who do you think you are, a noblewoman or something? In the Land of Three Roses, only the aristocracy can have flowers in their names. You ought to know that."

"Oh, I didn't know it, ma'am," Rosalie said, breaking into a sudden smile. "I didn't know that at all. I haven't been properly educated, I'm afraid."

"I'll call you Beetle," the old woman said. "That's a good name for a girl who's going to be sleeping among the potatoes. Don't just stand there like a puddinghead," she continued, pushing Rosalie aside roughly.

"But where should I go, ma'am?" Rosalie asked. "I've never been here before."

The old woman tossed her a glance of utter disgust. "Follow me," she said crossly. "Already you've been a thousand times more trouble than you're worth." She crossed the room and went out through another tumbledown door at the rear of the dwelling. Rosalie followed and found herself in a little shed made out of logs without any plaster to cover up the chinks. But at least if

71

rain and wind came into the shed, so did light and air which, Rosalie could immediately see, gave it a marked advantage over the rest of the cottage. There was a pile of filthy rags in one corner. Mrs. Limberger pointed to it and said with a sneer, "Your bed, milady. Poke through it and you'll find an old dress of my daughter's you can change into. It won't be any too clean—she's had no one to attend to her in a long time, poor thing, and she has so much on her mind. But at least it'll be dry. And then you can give me back that jacket, and you can give me the dress you're wearing, too. Fancy folk over to Rose-hilde is always giving their hand-me-downs to those as don't deserve them, while the rest of us can scarcely afford a potato sack. Your dress cleaned up some will do very well for my Odora to wear to Romana Roquefort's wedding." Mrs. Limberger's talon-like fingers grabbed Rosalie's skirt and rubbed the material possessively. "That fool Muenster Myost will turn green when he sees Odora looking like a fine lady," she muttered. "He'll be sorry he picked that witless Romana over my Odora, and serve him right, it will."

Rosalie offered no objection. The dress, even torn and soiled, obviously did not belong to a kitchen slavey, and the sooner she got out of it, the better off she'd be, at least for the time being.

They'd been expecting her, that was for sure, so for the present the wisest course seemed to try to be what they wanted her to be.

When the woman left her, Rosalie did not put on one of the rags, but taking a hint from the woman's remark about sacks, she found one lying among the potatoes and onions that were stored in the shed. It was an empty flour sack and though it wasn't much cleaner than the rags, Rosalie felt its dirt to be somewhat more bearable than the dirt of someone else's cast-offs. A door in the back wall of the shed led to the outside yard, and there Rosalie shook out the sack before she put it on. Later on, when she had a chance, she'd find another one and wash each one in the pool while wearing the other. Then they wouldn't be so bad, not so bad at all. After that she'd take a broom and sweep out her shed and make a bed out of some of the rushes that she was sure must grow along the river somewhere.

But although she spent a lot of time down at the pool doing the wash, she never did find a spare minute to go out looking for rushes to sleep on. From the very moment the old woman had come back into the shed to take away the green plaid gown, Rosalie had not had one second to herself, except when she slept. And by the time she was allowed to retire to the corner of her shed, she was so exhausted she couldn't begin to care whether the pile of rags she slept on was clean or dirty. It had not taken long for her to come to look like what she was, with her hair no longer wound neatly around her head in a coronet of braids, but hanging down her back in dirty clumps of knots, like abandoned birds' nests. Her face was always filthy, there were dark circles under her huge blue eyes, and each week she lost another pound or two. She ate after she finished serving the elder Limbergers and Odora, and they saw to it that there was never anything more than a crust or two of bread left for her meal.

Besides doing all the cleaning, cooking, washing, sewing, candle- and soap-making around the cottage, Rosalie had to take care of the chickens and ducks and keep the master's fishing gear in good repair for all the fish he never caught, as well as tend to the vegetable garden, which grew more weeds than anything else. The worst task of all was waiting on Odora who spent all of her time in bed, where her meals had to be served to her. Rosalie actually had to dress Odora completely on those rare occasions when she left her bed to go walking in the evening with some slovenly village lad who came by with a fistful of dank flowers in his hand and a gruesome leer in his eye. The second day Rosalie was at the Limbergers', the old lady said to her, "Beetle, you must bathe Odora today. She's beginning to smell.

Now that you're here, you can do it at least once a week. I haven't been able to get to it in the last month or two, I've been that busy."

"No, ma'am," Rosalie said firmly, "I will not bathe Odora. She's certainly big enough to bathe herself!"

Mrs. Limberger's usually white face turned red as fire. "How dare you talk back to me, you lazy creature? I knew you were worthless the moment I laid eyes on you, but I'll take care of you, indeed I will." And she picked up the broom that stood in the corner by the fireplace and chased after Rosalie, waving it frantically. Rosalie ran out through the door, and right into the arms of Mr. Limberger, who held her while his wife beat her about the legs and shoulders with the broom handle.

"Don't try any such tricks again," the old man said when his wife was done. "If she can't catch you, you can be sure that Odora or I will. Odora is pretty strong and pretty fast when she chooses to be."

Rosalie didn't say a word. She didn't even cry. She resolved then and there to suffer no more beatings, but to run away at the first opportunity, whether she was supposed to be at the Limbergers' or not. But there was no chance in the daytime to run away since one or the other of them had an eye on her every second, and she was too exhausted after hours of hard labor and scarcely any food to attempt an escape at night. Once she crept into her bed of rags, she never woke again until she heard Mrs. Limberger's harsh cry, "Wake up, Beetle, wake up, you lazy good-for-nothing." And so, to avoid any more physical punishment, she did exactly as she was told, and waited. Sometimes, in the one minute between the time she lay down and the time she fell asleep, she called silently for the Voice of the tower to return to her and tell her what to do now, but the Voice never answered.

One day her chance came. The Limbergers went off to the long-anticipated wedding of Romana Roquefort and Muenster Myost. They were very excited about going. "There hasn't been a real party in our section of County Blackrose in nearly a year," Odora confided as Rosalie combed her hair. It was more than she'd had the energy to say to Rosalie since the girl had come. "We hardly have any visitors, either. We're all so afraid of running into one of Count Blackrose's thieving soldiers, we scarcely go anywhere."

"Thieving is right," Mr. Limberger complained. "Last year I had to give them a quarter of what I grew, and this year I hear they're going to take a third. For protection, they say. Protection from whom? From them, of course. When will the Third Rose come? That's what I want to know. Haven't we waited and suffered long enough?"

"The Third Rose?" Rosalie asked. "What does that mean? What's the Third Rose?"

"Oh, Beetle, you puddinghead," Mrs. Limberger interrupted, "how can anyone be so stupid?"

"I told you," Rosalie explained patiently, "I've been badly educated."

"This is the Land of Three Roses," Mrs. Limberger said. "You know that much, don't you, little idiot?"

Rosalie nodded.

"Well, that's a mercy anyhow," the woman continued with a snort. "What we all want to know is —where is the Third Rose? Where is the Third Rose?" she repeated, her voice rising. "All the old books say that the Third Rose will come to break a tyrant's power."

"How do you know what the old books say?" Odora sneered. "You can't read."

"Everyone knows," her mother replied, "except dummies who don't keep their ears open, like you and Beetle. Count Blackrose knows it best of all. The Third Rose has to be of royal blood, and the royal line has grown so thin, only the King and the Count are left. The King has no children, and we've all heard that the Count murders his at birth, just to make sure. They say he even murders any child who has the bad luck to show the royal eyes or the royal skin," she added, her eyes quickly sliding over Rosalie's freckled face.

"Why, that's frightful," Rosalie cried with a shudder.

"It's discouraging anyway," Mrs. Limberger went on, her face a gloomy mask. "The Third Rose will never come. Count Blackrose and that witch Liederkranz who does all his dirty work for him will see to that!"

"Oh, let's not think about things like that today," Odora said. "Today we're supposed to enjoy ourselves for once. I want to go now. If we're late, all the food will be gone." She rose heavily from her seat and turned herself around in a ghastly imitation of a pirouette. "How do I look?" she asked with a simper. Rosalie had the satisfaction of knowing that Odora looked perfectly ridiculous in the green plaid dress, though of course she didn't say so. Odora couldn't even button the dress across her enormous bosom, and it fell barely to her knees. As a result, she seemed to be wearing a petticoat somewhat unexpectedly trimmed in green plaid, and nothing more.

"Beetle," Mrs. Limberger said before she left, "while we're gone, you can take Odora's mattress and blankets out into the yard and give them a good airing. You can clean out the chicken coops and the duck pens, you can weed the garden, and you can sweep and mop all the floors. I'd have you start supper too, but with your appetite, I can't trust you near the food unless I'm watching you. Now, I don't think I've given you a single task you can't manage on your own, have I? How I got stuck with a charity girl who didn't even know how to make soap or candles when she came, I'll never know. The education I've given you, Beetle, is priceless, and I doubt you even appreciate it. But I've decided to pay you no wages. Apprentices are not entitled to wages."

Rosalie made no reply. "Drop me a curtsy when I speak to you, Beetle," the woman insisted. "Don't just stand there like a dummy, even if you are one."

Rosalie curtsied, and the woman seemed satisfied for the moment. They left then, and Rosalie resolved to give them a half hour's head start and then be on her way herself. Bread and meat were locked in a food safe to which she had no key, but she meant to help herself to all the potatoes and onions she could carry, and to some flint and tinder too, to make a fire. To take such things would not be stealing, she felt sure, since she knew perfectly well that for the amount of work she had done, she was well entitled to wages. This time she would be better prepared for her journey, and would not be forced to stop with the first people who were willing to take her in, regardless of how horrid they might turn out to be.

She tied up some potatoes, onions, candles, soap, and the tinder box in one of the old rags she'd been sleeping on. She was strongly tempted to take the sheepskin coat too, but decided that perhaps that *would* be stealing. The Limbergers had sheltered her, after all, and fed her too, in a fashion. She just dressed herself in as many rags and sacks as she could, so she'd have something with which to keep herself warm at night, and then she picked up her bundle and left the cottage. She headed straight for the stream, intending to bathe in the pool so that she could begin her journey clean and feeling more like her old self.

She clambered down the rocky path, raising the dry dust in the thick, silent summer heat as she went. When she reached the green coolness of the tree-shrouded pool, she jumped in with all her rags on her back. They'd dry in the sun as she walked, and then they'd be clean too, for the first time since they'd entered the Limberger cottage countless years before. She was splashing around quite happily in the water, when all of a sudden she heard the sound of heavy footsteps crashing through the brush. Fearful that one of the Limbergers might be returning home for some unexpected reason, she scrambled for the bank as quickly as she could. But it was not Old Man Limberger or Old Lady Limberger or Odora she met as she climbed out of the water.

It was a great brown bear.

Ring around a rosy,
Pocket full of posies,
Ashes, ashes,
We all fall down.

Tex sang that baby rhyme as I walked into the bar. He sang softly, but I could hear him. As he sang, he rubbed the top of the bar with a soft old napkin stained with furniture oil.

I interrupted his song. "Listen, Tex," I said, "what do you think my chances are?"

Tex answered with another question. "Your chances of what, Princess?"

"Of getting a dog for my birthday."

"I'd get you a dog myself," Tex said, "if your mother would let you keep it."

"You didn't answer my question, Tex. What do you think my chances are?"

He looked up from his work. The bar top was already so shiny you could see your face in it. "I think I did answer it," he said.

I sighed. "No chance at all." I gave the blue leather side of the bar a good kick. What I really wanted to kick was the whole Waterbridge Inn.

I climbed down off my bar stool. "Hey, where're you going, Princess?" Tex asked. "We haven't figured out what's going on in the Land of Three Roses today."

"I'll come back later," I said. I wandered through the lobby, down the hall, past the checkroom, and into the kitchen. Luke was chopping carrots with a broad-blade French knife. He cut four peeled carrots into forty tiny pieces in four seconds. I could hardly see the knife blade move. Every time I watched him do it, I was afraid he'd cut off a piece of his finger. I couldn't take my eyes off his hands as he chopped, but I was always glad when he was done. He did have slices missing from his left index finger and his thumb. He said it was a hazard of the trade. He said you'd hardly find a chef who wasn't in a similar fix. But it had happened long ago, he said, when he was young and careless, and liked to show off.

"Luke," I said, "Mom listens to you. She has a lot of respect for you."

"I hope so," Luke replied calmly. He stopped his

chopping and looked at me. He knew something was coming.

"Luke, I gotta have a dog. I really do. I'll go bats if I don't get a dog."

"You've got Buster," Luke said.

"I don't have Buster," I replied sharply. "Buster isn't mine. If I had my own dog, you think I'd treat him the way Mrs. Dunleigh treats Buster? I don't want a dog to be my baby. I want a dog to be my friend."

"You have a lot of friends," Luke replied as he began his chop, chop, chopping again.

"No, I don't," I insisted. "The girls in my class are a bunch of snobs. There was one boy who was my friend for a little while, but he turned out to be a real louse. So now I have no friends at all."

"What about me?" Luke asked. "What about Min? What about Tex?"

"Luke," I said, "be honest. Are you going to go outside and play with me? Even Tex doesn't do that. Besides, did you know that Buster has a heart condition? Mrs. Dunleigh told me. He's going to die soon. That's why he snuffles all the time. He can hardly breathe."

"I'm sorry to hear that about Buster," Luke replied, "but he's an old dog. We all gotta go sometime."

"Yeah, but when he goes, I won't even have Buster. Don't you understand that?"

"I understand," Luke said, "but I understand your

84

mother too. It wouldn't do to have a dog running around this place. He'd come in here, and we'd end up with dog hair in the soup. The Board of Health wouldn't go for that, I can tell you."

"I'd train him to stay out of the kitchen. Don't you worry about that. I've read every dog-training book in the library. I've read every dog book, period, even the ones in the grown-up section."

But like Mom, Luke wasn't listening. He was running along his own track. "And then the exterminator comes every month and puts rat poison down in all the corners. Now, a dog would get hold of that stuff and he'd be dead in ten minutes. You can't expect some new puppy to behave like Buster. Mrs. Dunleigh carries Buster most places, and when she's not carrying him, he's not more than six inches from her heels. A puppy would be into everything, doing his business in the dining room, chewing up the booths in the bar. What do you think the Board of Health would say to that?"

"You weren't listening to me, Luke," I said. "I told you, I'd train him. I know all about it."

Luke swept the little pieces of carrot into a big soup pot. "The girls in school," he said, "they'll be your friends again soon. This is just a passing thing. These girl quarrels never last very long."

I felt the tears well up in my eyes. "Girl quarrels." What a stupid thing to say.

I walked away from him and opened the door to the

cellar. Pedro was coming up the steep, narrow steps carrying a cardboard carton piled high with lettuce, tomatoes, cucumbers, carrots, and celery. Sylvester was behind him with another one. I waited until they came up into the kitchen and then I ran down the steps with my hand on the rail. Once I'd twisted my leg and fallen down those steps, hitting every single one as I went. I had screamed all the way down, and when I got to the bottom, I went on screaming. Everyone came running, even Mom. My leg hurt so much, I was sure it was broken. Mom rushed me to the emergency room at the hospital, and they X-rayed me, but I was just badly bruised. I didn't get my leg in a cast, or piles of cards and presents, or anything like that.

The cellar had lots of rooms. After all, it was as big as the main floor. It had a soda and beer room, a butcher shop, a liquor room, a storeroom for canned goods, a storeroom for paper goods, and a room where Sylvester and Pedro peeled the potatoes and onions that were kept there in big bags. It had two big walk-in refrigerators. It even had a toilet and a locker room for the help.

But the best thing about the cellar was its long cement-floored hall where Rachel, Dan, and I roller-skated. We kept our skates under the wooden table in the butcher shop. The skate keys were on a little nail hammered into the table leg. Rachel's and Dan's were covered with dust. They hadn't used them in a long time. I guess I hadn't used mine in a long time either.

Like customer-watching from the top of the steps, skating alone wasn't much fun.

But I felt like I was a tiger in a cage. The cage was my own skin. I had to move. It was raining, and I couldn't run around outside, so I put on my skates. I skated out of the butcher shop, into the hall, and up and down the hall as fast as I could go.

Then I decided to skate in and out of each room that wasn't padlocked. In and out of the butcher shop, in and out of the locker room, in the potato room—but not out.

I stopped just inside the potato room door to turn on the light. I didn't want to fall on any sacks or big pots Sylvester might have left in the middle of the floor. I heard a faint little squeaking sound and when I looked in the corner from which the noise seemed to come, I saw a tiny little mouse, a baby mouse. He was so small he didn't have the sense to run away from the light or from me. He just stood there in the corner, squeaking.

I didn't want to make any loud noise that would frighten the mouseling. You can't be quiet on roller skates, so I bent over and very carefully took mine off. Luckily, I had the key in my pocket.

I tiptoed over to where the mouse stood. He was shivering. How had he gotten here? Where was his mother? Why had she abandoned him? He would die if I left him here. He would starve to death. He was too frightened to move. He was actually paralyzed with fright.

87

I knelt down very, very quietly. Very, very slowly I reached out my hand and picked up the mouseling. I cupped my palm and held him there, very, very carefully. It was warm in my hand and soon he stopped shivering. He liked it better there than on the floor.

I went back up the cellar stairs and into the kitchen to show my mouse to Tex. But when I got upstairs, I found that my mother was in the kitchen. I thought I would put the mouse in my pocket, and just walk right through the swinging doors, into the Holiday Room, out into the lobby, and then upstairs. In my room, I could find a shoe box for the mouseling to live in. Mom wouldn't ever know.

But it was too late. Mom saw me. "Oh, Rosie," she said, "I've been looking for you." She walked toward me. "We're going to put up the Christmas decorations now. I know you like doing that." She put her hand on my arm and smiled. "This year it's your turn to decide the color scheme for the tree, you know." Then the smile disappeared. "What's that?" she asked. "What's that in your hand?"

I opened my palm. "A mouse," I said. I tried to speak in the same kind of voice I would have used to say "A stone" or "A pencil." I stroked the mouseling with my finger. "I'm going to keep him in a box in my room, for a pet."

"Oh, Rosie, Rosie," my mother said, "you can't keep a mouse for a pet. Mice are dirty. I pay the exterminator seven dollars a month to get rid of mice!"

"But this is a baby," I protested. "He'll die if I don't feed him."

Mom looked at me for a minute without saying anything. Then she spoke very softly. "Rosie, honey," she said with a little laugh, "that's the whole idea."

"For him to die?" I was shocked.

My mother nodded and shrugged her shoulders. "That's the way it is, babe," she said. "The Board of Health would close us down in a minute if they thought we were infested with mice."

"Look, Mom, I'll keep him in a shoe box. Any mess he makes will be right in there, where I can clean it up."

"He'll chew his way through a box in two seconds flat," my mother replied.

"I'll find a metal box. I'll make holes in the top of it with a beer can opener." I was desperate.

"Absolutely not, Rosie. Absolutely not. We'd be able to smell him all over the building. Anyway, how long do you think he'd survive under such conditions?"

"But, Mom," I cried, "what am I going to do with him? I won't let you kill him. I won't."

"Take him outside," Mom suggested. "Let him loose in the back field."

"But that's killing him," I said. "It's the same thing as killing him."

"No, it's not," she insisted. "He'll have a chance."

"Mom, I can't do that. I can't."

"Then I'll do it," she said sharply. She reached out her hand. She would have crushed him. "All right," I gave in. "All right. I'll put him outside."

"That's being sensible," Mom said. "I know you can be a sensible girl when you want to be." Then she walked out of the kitchen.

My eyes were so full of tears I couldn't see. But I didn't walk through the outside door. I went downstairs, back to the potato room. "Goodbye, Mouseling," I whispered as I kissed him on top of his head. I put him down in the corner where I'd first seen him. Maybe there his mother would find him again. Then I shut the light and went away.

In the upstairs hall, I met my mother again. She didn't even ask about the mouse. She'd forgotten him already. She was carrying a dozen boxes of Christmas lights that she had brought down from the attic. "Rosie," she said, "go on up; there's a big cardboard carton right at the top of the steps. I couldn't manage everything at once. Carry it down to the lobby. I'll send Sylvester up for the rest of the stuff."

She didn't notice that my face was simply ravaged by tears. I clumped up into the attic making as much noise as I could. She didn't notice that either. She was already gone. I found the cardboard box. I thought maybe I'd drop it, so that all the Christmas balls would break, and she'd have to go downtown to buy more. But I didn't drop it. I loved those big fat balls too much to do that. This year I'd do the tree entirely in pink and gold. Then within those balls I could see our lobby, the whole lobby in each ball, no longer dim and shabby, but gleaming in rose and gold like a fairyland palace.

Sylvester was carrying the tree into the lobby just as I got there. Tex, who was very tall, had come in to hang the strings of lights which Rachel and Dan were pulling out of the boxes Mom had carried down. Even Dan helped decorate the tree. It was funny—we were Jewish, we didn't celebrate Christmas, yet we put up more Christmas decorations than anyone else in town. We did it for the customers. The Inn would be jammed each night for the next three weeks with holiday parties.

I loved putting up those decorations. I loved helping Mom wrap the bottles of liquor she gave each year to good customers. I loved cutting cartoons and pictures out of magazines for the funny place cards she made for the Inn's own Christmas party. Rachel had told me that before the war, we'd had our own tree and presents on Christmas morning. But the war had made Mom much more Jewish than she had been before. That was because of what Hitler did to the Jews. Rachel said it was a good thing we didn't get Christmas presents anymore. She said it was important to know who you were, and you shouldn't try to be something else. But still, I was glad we had a little piece of Christmas.

It certainly didn't make up for Mouseling, though. I thought about him the whole time I was trimming the tree. Once I got down from my ladder and went to the

91

cellar. I turned the light on in the potato room, but Mouseling wasn't there. I would never know what had happened to him.

I went back to my work. I hung more and more pink and gold balls on the tree. After a while, Rachel and Dan drifted off somewhere. Then some people came in to talk about a wedding and Mom went with them into her office. "Be careful, Rosie," she called as she left. "You hung that ball too close to the end of the branch. It may fall off. Move it back." My mother didn't know anything about me. She didn't know one single thing.

Only Tex and I were left to trim the tree. We talked about the Land of Three Roses while we worked.

So startled was Rosalie at the sight of the huge, hairy bear that appeared suddenly between two willows, she almost fell back into the water. The bear reached out a huge paw and grabbed her by her makeshift skirt. "Don't go," he said. "Please don't go. I've been anxious to meet you. That's why I showed myself today."

He spoke so pleasantly, so politely, in a deep, warm voice, that Rosalie found it hard to be afraid. "You knew I was here?" she asked.

"Oh, yes," he said, loosening his grip on her skirt. "I know a lot."

"Do you know who I am?"

"Yes," he answered, raising himself up on his hind legs. "Old Mrs. Limberger calls you Beetle, but you're really Rosalie."

"That's right," she said, and any lingering fear of him she might have felt disappeared entirely. "Who are you?"

"The Old One," he replied solemnly.

"The one Mr. Limberger hates? The one who steals all the fish out of the pond? Oh, I am glad to meet you, too. So glad."

"I don't steal the fish," the bear replied with dignity. "The fish belong to me. I was here long before Limberger, or any other human being, for that matter. It's Limberger who does the stealing."

"Don't worry about it," Rosalie assured him. "He hasn't caught a fish in ages. Not since I've been here, anyway, and that's two or three weeks. I'm not quite sure. I'm afraid I've rather lost track of time."

The bear scrutinized her carefully. "You have let yourself go, haven't you? Do you think that was so wise?"

"Oh, I just couldn't manage to keep clean," Rosalie apologized. "This is the cleanest I've been since I came. They didn't give me a minute to myself. But I'm leaving now, and I'll be better able to take care of things."

93

"Leaving?" the Old One queried. "Why are you doing that?"

"Being here is hardly any better than being in my tower," Rosalie complained. "Do you know about my tower?"

The Old One nodded.

"Do you know why I was there, or who my Voice was?"

"That's for you to find out," the bear replied.

"Well, how can I here, any more than I could when I was there?"

The Old One shrugged his hairy shoulders. "Then leave," he said. "Perhaps that is the wisest course. You must do what you think is right. Of course, they were expecting you."

"Yes," Rosalie replied. "Do you think that means something?"

The Old One shrugged again. "Maybe it does, and maybe it doesn't."

"Do you think I ought to stick around and find out?" Rosalie asked, feeling her heart sink down into her stomach.

"That's for you to decide," the Old One announced heavily.

"A lot of help you are," Rosalie said with a frown. She stood silently for a moment, twisting her hair around her finger as she thought. "They took me in," she said finally, "but that's no big deal. Look at all I've done for them. Their place

94

is clean for the first time in heaven knows how long. I don't owe them a thing."

"That is as it may be," the Old One said.

"I don't really mind working," Rosalie continued slowly. "I've learned a lot. I don't like being a slave, but I'm glad I know how to manage for myself now."

"That's worth a lot," the Old One pontificated.

"Look here," Rosalie queried, "do all bears talk? I thought only people could talk. The chickens and ducks in the Limbergers' yard can't talk."

"Most birds are fools," the Old One replied. "But bears can talk if they want to. Usually they don't want to."

"What about other animals?" Rosalie asked.

"What do you want, all natural history in five minutes?" the Old One asked, more than a little crossly. "There's time enough for that later on."

"I guess I'd better stay," Rosalie said. "If I leave, I might never see you again."

"And then think what you'd miss," the bear said, quite seriously. "Since you're going to stay," he added, "I'll see to it that you get enough to eat, you can be sure."

"Do you really mean that?" Rosalie asked. "Can I really believe you?"

The bear drew himself up to his full height, which was about nine feet. Rosalie could not help but be impressed. "No one," he said with dignity, "no one has ever doubted my word before."

"I'm sorry, sir," Rosalie assured him hastily. "Please forgive me."

"It's understandable," he relented a bit, "considering what you've gone through. But don't you see, you can always run away later. If I fail you, then you can leave. You'll have lost nothing."

"Except another five pounds or so," Rosalie said.

"You can afford it," the bear pointed out. "Besides, I told you. I'll take care of that."

Rosalie stared down into the water of the pool. Before, when she was bathing, the level of the pond had risen no farther than her waist, but now as she looked into it, she could not see the bottom, even though the water was as clear as glass. It was teeming with fish, all kinds of fish, in all shapes, sizes, and colors, yet Rosalie had heard Mr. Limberger complain dozens of times that all the fish were gone from the pool. "All right," she said as she gazed at flashing fins and shiny scales, "I've definitely made up my mind. I'll stay. For a while, anyhow. If things don't work out, I'll leave next time there's a wedding. It's summer; there's bound to be another one before long." She glanced up at her friend again.

"When will I see you? How will I see you?"

"I'll come when it suits me," the bear told her. "And how I'll come is up to me too. But mark my words. You won't go to sleep hungry again. And no one will beat you either."

"Not even if I refuse to bathe Odora?"

"Odora," the bear snorted, "is old enough to bathe herself."

"Exactly," Rosalie replied.

"Do the work that can legitimately be expected of a kitchen maid," the bear said. "Don't do any more."

"How do I know what that work is?" Rosalie asked.

"I think," the Old One responded, "I can leave that to your own good judgment." He turned away from Rosalie and lumbered down to the water's edge and waded into the pool. He reached out a paw, and two fish leapt into it. One he ate immediately. The other he presented to Rosalie. "Your dinner," he said. And then, without another word, he disappeared through the green willow branches. Both the sight and sound of him were gone before Rosalie had a chance to ask even one of the thousand questions that were on the tip of her tongue.

She built a fire and roasted a potato, an onion, and the fish for her dinner. It was the first time she'd been full since she had left her tower, and the food she had just eaten tasted infinitely more delicious than anything that had ever been presented to her by those invisible magic hands which once had served her so faithfully. She drank some water from the pool and then she fell asleep. A late afternoon chill awakened her, and she realized that her golden day was nearly over. She had to get back before the Limbergers. They would be furious enough when they returned and found none of the work they had assigned her even started, let alone done. The Old One's promise that no one would beat her again would soon be put to the test.

As Rosalie came up the sandy path which led from the pool to the clearing in which the cottage stood, she was greeted by a sight even more startling than that of the great bear lumbering through the willow trees. Odora was not at the wedding. She was at home and she was sweeping! She was sweeping the hard-baked dirt in front of the door-step and screaming at the chickens, "Get out of here, you stinking birds. Get out of here."

Rosalie couldn't imagine what had happened to bring Odora back to the cottage before midnight. It was only sunset; the wedding celebration was scarcely underway. But even more amazing was the sight of Odora's enormous bulk, still clad in her good petticoat and the green

98

plaid gown, flailing away with the broom—to no avail, as might be expected.

"So there you are, Beetle," Odora cried as she caught sight of her. "Wherever have you been?"

"Washing potatoes and onions in the pool," Rosalie replied calmly. "Here, give me that broom. You don't know what to do with it. Put these vegetables back into the shed." With a motion so swift that Odora had no opportunity to object, and even less reason, Rosalie traded her bundle for the broom and set about chasing the fowl into their coops and setting the yard to rights. She had just swept the last bit of dung into the vegetable garden when Mrs. Limberger came out of the cottage, hammer and nails in hand.

"Oh, my goodness," she cried when she set eyes on Rosalie. "Beetle, thank heavens you're here." She seemed less angry than relieved at the sight of her. "Where have you been, girl, where have you been?"

"Sweeping the yard, ma'am," Rosalie replied.

"Well, see if you can fix this hinge. Do something, anyway, so that the door doesn't look as if it's going to fall down on the head of the first person who walks through."

"Certainly, ma'am," Rosalie agreed. She took the hammer and the nails from Mrs. Limberger and handed her the broom, which the woman took from her without a murmur. "Might I ask what's going on?" Rosalie inquired politely. "It must be something quite remarkable if Miss Odora actually went so far as to pick up a broom."

"Count Blackrose was at the wedding," Mrs. Limberger said. "Can you imagine that?"

"No, ma'am, indeed I cannot," Rosalie replied as she hammered away at the broken hinge. "What was the greatest lord in the kingdom doing at Romana Roquefort's wedding?"

"Count Blackrose's dead wife's third cousin married a wealthy Roquefort who made a lot of money in Terrarosa, canning sardines. That's why those Roqueforts put on such airs. Now that Count Blackrose has condescended to attend the wedding, Mrs. Roquefort will be more impossible than ever. But when she hears the real reason Count Blackrose came into our district, she won't put on such airs any longer. And I shall make sure she hears of it, never fear."

"And what is that, if I may ask?" Rosalie said as she swung the door neatly shut.

"Oh, you stupid Beetle," Mrs. Limberger said, "do you think we'd be running around here like headless chickens just because Count Blackrose was at the Roquefort wedding? He's coming here, you silly child, don't you understand? He's coming here!"

"That monster here?" Rosalie exclaimed, her

100

calm self-control shattered. "How terrible!"

"Terrible, puddinghead, terrible?" Mrs. Limberger replied impatiently. "It'll be the making of us, you idiot. Whether Count Blackrose is a tyrant or not won't matter to us anymore!"

"That's what you think," Mr. Limberger announced as he came round the edge of the cottage carrying his fishing poles in his hand. "When the Count gets to the pool, the famous pool he says he's heard so much about, and finds that there isn't a fish in it any bigger than a minnow, he's going to have all our heads. I curse the day I was born, and you should too, my fine lady, if you have a grain of sense."

"Oh, you fool," cried the woman, "you poor blind fool. Do you believe, do you really believe Count Blackrose is coming here to fish in a pool where there are no fish? He's a famous sportsman, I know. He may have come into our district for that originally, but one glance at our Odora pushed any thought of fish out of his head. I could see it the moment he stepped foot into the village church. It was as plain as the nose on your face."

"Odora? Odora?" Mr. Limberger put his head back and roared with laughter. "That's the most ridiculous thing I've ever heard. Absolutely the most ridiculous thing I've heard in my whole life. Odora's about as attractive as a sow. What

101

would a man who's accustomed to the dainty beauties of the court at Rosehilde want with the likes of our Odora?"

"Everyone to his own taste," Mrs. Limberger sniffed. "Sometimes these aristocratic gentlemen get tired of what's always at hand and want something different to stir up their jaded appetites."

"She's different," the old man snorted. "They don't come any differenter than her, that's for sure."

"You'd think you were talking about a stranger instead of your own daughter," Mrs. Limberger scolded. "No one's saying Count Blackrose is going to marry her. But he's interested, I know, and whatever he wants, he'll pay for. He'll set us up for the rest of our lives, if we handle this right. Now, Beetle," she added almost kindly, so happy was she in her dream of her daughter's imminent social success, "go in and clean Odora up a bit. I'll take care of putting the house in order."

Rosalie was more than a little shocked that Mrs. Limberger could so coolly contemplate handing her daughter over to a man who was rumored to have murdered his own children, but she said nothing. She walked into the house, and then paused as she overheard the old man's next remark. He was trying to whisper, but he really didn't know how. Since the conversation was about her, Rosalie felt no qualms about listening.

"It's not Odora Count Blackrose is after," Mr. Limberger said, "and it's hit me that he's not after any disappearing fish, either. It's the one that was sent to us he's coming to see, and there'll be hell to pay when he finds her looking like something the cat dragged in. If I were you, I'd forget about Odora and see to it that Beetle's wearing the dress she came in when Count Blackrose shows up."

As soon as the old woman started arguing with him, Rosalie hurried away to Odora. She repaired Odora's petticoat and the green plaid dress where they had ripped, and she washed Odora's face and combed her hair. "Now, Odora," she ordered, "you go sit on the bench by the front door and don't move until Count Blackrose gets here. Your mother and I will finish cleaning up." Rosalie knew that if Odora did anything more than remain absolutely motionless, she'd instantly look a mess again. Even sitting still was no guarantee that some blob of dirt wouldn't fall from the heavens and land smack in the middle of her skirt or her nose, but all anyone could do to prevent that was pray.

Odora obeyed. "I'll just pick myself a few flowers," she simpered, "and then I'll sit on the bench looking just as pretty as I know how. Count Blackrose can't help noticing me."

"You're right about that," Rosalie agreed. She followed Odora to the door and watched her as she stepped outside, in case she tripped. Then she turned to help Mrs. Limberger, who was doing her best to straighten out the room.

"I can manage here," the woman said grudgingly. "You go clean yourself up too. You're no credit to us, the way you look now. People would think we mistreated you or something."

"My face is clean, ma'am," Rosalie said. "My hair is combed. What else can I do? I have nothing to wear but what I have on."

The old woman hesitated a moment, and then she said so softly Rosalie could barely hear her, "Take your dress back from Odora."

"No, thanks," Rosalie said, scarcely able to conceal a shiver of disgust. "I think it's too late anyway," she added, and sure enough, as the two of them stood silent for a moment, listening, they could hear the clatter of horses' hooves on the road that ran across the hilltop above the cottage. Immediately they went out into the yard, where Mr. Limberger stood like a soldier at attention, presenting his fishing poles instead of arms, and Odora sat on the bench, a doltish smile on her face, her skirts spread about her in what she took to be a graceful arrangement, and her eyelashes fluttering so furiously that Rosalie feared they might fall off before Count Blackrose made it down the hill.

But he didn't take long. In a moment four outriders seemed to fill the clearing. They were dressed in such magnificent black uniforms, trimmed in gold and rose braid, that Rosalie would have been sure one of them was the Count if he had come alone. Blackrose, when he did appear, was something of a disappointment, though he rode a magnificent roan horse which cast the mounts of his servants well into the shade. But he himself wore plain black riding clothes and black boots, with a white shirt and the simplest of white neckcloths. He was no longer young, and his reddish-brown hair and beard were grizzled with gray. His soldiers had dismounted before he clattered into the clearing. They held his horse while he jumped from the saddle with agility. Mr. Limberger bowed low, and his wife and Rosalie made deep curtsies which they held as he approached them. Only Odora remained seated on the bench, sniffing the bunch of dandelions she had picked as if she held a nosegay of rosebuds and violets.

Count Blackrose paid no attention to her at all. He headed straight for the three standing near the door. "You may rise," he said coldly. As she did so, Rosalie looked up into his face and was startled to see large blue eyes, fringed with heavy lashes, exactly like hers, except that they were as hard and icy as two pieces of agate.

Count Blackrose looked at Rosalie as directly

as she looked at him. Every bit of blood drained from his face as he stared at her, and he was as white as if he had seen a ghost. "Who is this child?" he asked harshly.

"Beetle, our serving wench, sire," Mrs. Limberger explained hesitantly.

"Don't call me 'sire,'" Blackrose corrected her. "Only the King is called 'sire.' 'Sir' will do well enough for me—for now."

"I'm sorry, sir," Mrs. Limberger corrected herself humbly. "Indeed I am."

"How dare this child have freckles?" Count Blackrose asked as he stared again at Rosalie through narrowed eyes. "You all know that in the Land of Three Roses, only the children of the aristocracy have freckles."

"We're sorry she has freckles, sir, indeed we are, sir," Mr. Limberger replied, bowing and scraping, scraping and bowing all the while that he spoke.

"Stop bobbing about like that, man," Count Blackrose said. "You're making me sick. You'll be punished for this, you know. You'll be punished for a harboring a child with freckles. It's strictly against the law."

"She's not ours, sir," the woman said hastily. "She was sent to us. We had no choice but to take her in."

"Motive is no excuse if a crime is committed.

You know that, woman." His voice was as hard and flat as his eyes.

Rosalie could control herself no longer. "But that's absurd. Master and mistress can't help it if I have freckles, and I can't either."

"Bleach, my girl, bleach. You should have bleached them away. It was your obligation."

"Out here, sir," the woman tried to explain, "no one ever sees her. No one ever comes here. We didn't give it a thought."

"Give her to me," Count Blackrose said. "I'll see to it that those freckles are removed from her face soon enough, you can be sure."

The Limbergers began to tremble. It was clear that they were more frightened than they had ever been in their lives. So was Rosalie. The Limbergers were bad enough, but to be delivered into the power of Count Blackrose would be infinitely worse, she was sure. Besides, she was furious with the Old One. He should have urged her to leave. Now she had lost her chance.

But if the Limbergers were afraid of Count Blackrose, they were equally afraid of something else. For some reason which was utterly beyond Rosalie's comprehension, they were not about to give her up easily. "Oh, I'd like to give her to you, sir," the woman said, "indeed I would. She's a troublesome, disobedient girl, more bother than she's worth. But I can't. It's not permitted. The

107

paper, sir, the paper says we must keep her, and if we don't, great harm will come to us."

"Even greater harm will come to you if you don't give her up," Count Blackrose said. "I can guarantee that. Let me see that paper. It probably isn't even legal. Remember, in this district I rule. What they say at the court in Rosehilde cannot override my decree in County Blackrose—even if it comes from the hand of the King himself."

"Odora," the old man said, "go in the house and bring the box I keep in the hole next to the fireplace."

Odora looked startled at such an order. "Let Beetle go," she whined. "She's the servant, not me."

"Do as I say," her father thundered, and Odora scuttled away as quickly as her great bulk would allow. The others stood in silence in the dusty, shadeless clearing, while the evening shadows that came out of the woods grew longer and longer. When Odora came back with the box, her father unlocked it with a key he carried in the pocket of his trousers and withdrew a piece of parchment which he showed to the Count. "I can't read it, sir," he said. "I only know the man who brought it was dressed in the deep rose velvet livery of Rosehilde and he said I must not lose it, or the girl when she came, on pain of my life."

"He lied to you," Blackrose replied as he snatched the paper from Limberger's hand. He glanced over it quickly. "This paper is nothing but an old deed. That man probably wasn't from Rosehilde at all. He was nothing but some pitiful tradesman trying to get rid of a freckled-faced daughter who was beginning to prove an embarrassment. No doubt her freckles didn't respond to the bleaching process. But they will for me. You've heard the name of Liederkranz, haven't you?" he added, a grim smile appearing on his lips.

"Everyone's heard of the witch Liederkranz," Mr. Limberger replied, his voice scarcely more than a whisper.

"I haven't," Odora remarked. No one paid any attention to her, least of all the Count.

"Liederkranz now lives in my castle village," Blackrose said. "I imagine she'll know how to take care of a few freckles." He gestured sharply toward Rosalie. "Come along, girl, come along."

"The fishing, sir . . ." Limberger suggested tentatively.

"Don't speak unless you're spoken to," Count Blackrose interrupted. "I'll come back another day for the fishing. Come along, girl," he repeated.

"No," Rosalie replied. "I will not."

Count Blackrose turned on her a glance of

withering contempt. He waved toward two of his soldiers. "Seize her," he ordered. To the two remaining he shouted, "Take care of the others." The soldiers obeyed, and in a moment, Rosalie found herself seated on one of the horses in front of a man who held her two arms cruelly behind her back with one of his hands while he grasped the reins with the other. Accompanied by the screams and shouts of Mr. and Mrs. Limberger, who were also confined in the powerful grip of the remaining soldiers, they rode off through the clearing and into the woods. Of them all, only Odora remained calm, smiling her foolish smile, fluttering her eyelashes and sniffing her absurd bouquet.

Gather ye Rose-buds while ye may,
Old Time is still a flying:
And this same flower that smiles to day,
To morrow will be dying.

Rachel came in my room Saturday morning to show me
that poem. She had just read it in her English literature
book. She said it was by a man named Robert Herrick
who lived about three hundred years ago. "You know
what I'm going to do for your birthday?" Rachel said.
"I'm going to collect all the rose poems and rose sayings
I can find, and I'm going to write them out in my best
handwriting and put them together in a book for you."

"That'll be very nice," I said.

I guess I didn't sound too enthusiastic, because right
away Rachel added, "Of course, that won't be your only

present. It'll just be a little extra one." That meant besides making me a book, she'd buy me one. She always got Dan and me books for our birthdays. She was trying to make intellectuals out of us. She wasn't getting too far with Dan. The only things he liked to read were the sports pages and jazz magazines. But I usually liked the books Rachel bought me. As for the poetry—well, that was another matter. Still, the rosebud one was better than the other one, the one about a rose is a rose is a rose. That one didn't make any sense at all.

"Get me an animal book," I said. "Get me *My Friend Flicka*. That's a book I want to own. Or *National Velvet*."

"OK," Rachel said, "I'll see what I can do." Then her eyes glanced from one corner of my room to the other and she ordered, "Clean up this place. It looks like a pigsty." How could anyone be so nice one minute and so rotten the next?

"You're not my mother," I reminded her. "And you don't even know what a pigsty looks like. You've never seen one. Actually, pigs are very clean animals. They only roll around in the mud when there's nothing else to roll around in. They only eat slops when there's nothing else to eat."

"All right," Rachel replied, "so you know more about pigs than I do. Clean up your room anyway." She walked out, giving the door a good, hard slam as she left.

I didn't clean up my room. I certainly wasn't going to

do it just because she had told me to. I'd get around to it later, maybe. Instead, I went outside to get the mail. I always picked up the mail at eleven o'clock any morning that I was home. I liked getting mail, and I got a lot of it, too. I sent cereal box tops for anything that was free, and I entered every contest I saw in a magazine or newspaper or heard about on the radio. "I use Hinds Honey and Almond Cream because ——————. Complete the sentence in twenty-five words or less." I hadn't won anything yet, but I knew I would some day, and in the meantime, I often received a letter thanking me for my entry.

I riffled through the pile of checks, bills, and advertisements to see if there was anything for me. There was, and it wasn't a form letter from a manufacturer, either. The address was written out in ink. I put the other letters down on my mother's desk and opened the one that was for me. It was from Estelle Coviella. It was an invitation to her birthday party next Saturday. The invitation said it was going to be a luncheon party. Millie Van Dyke had only served ice cream and cake. Millie Van Dyke hadn't sent out written invitations, either. She had just asked people in school.

Mother wasn't in the kitchen or the Holiday Room. I went into the bar. She wasn't there either, but Tex was. "See, Tex," I said, holding out the invitation, "isn't this classy? It came in the mail."

Tex looked at it. "Very nice," he said. "When you get an invitation like that, you know in advance it's

113

going to be the kind of party where everything is done right."

I nodded my agreement as I climbed up on one of the bar stools. Tex was in that morning because there was to be a wedding reception at one o'clock and he had to serve the wedding guests their drinks. From September through December and again in May and June there were wedding receptions most Saturday afternoons.

"Do you want a Coke?" Tex asked me.

"No, thanks," I said. "I can't drink soda before lunch."

"In the south they do," Tex said. "In the south they have Coke with breakfast sometimes."

"How did you end up here, Tex," I asked him, "so far from where you began?"

"Just drifted around," he replied. "The Waterbridge Inn is the nearest thing to home I've known in years."

"You haven't been here all that long," I said. "Not like Luke or Min. They came right after Daddy died, and that was six years ago. We only came ourselves a year before that."

"Let's see," Tex said, counting on his fingers. "The war ended in '45 and I was out of the army nearly a year when I showed up here, so that was the beginning of '47. I've been here close to two years. That's a long time for me. You know, Princess, I'm like the tumble-weed down home. I just keep rolling along."

"I don't remember much from before Mom and

Dad bought the Inn and we moved here," I said. "We lived in a house, though. I know that. We were like ordinary people."

"Boring," Tex said. "Very boring."

"If I lived in a house I could have a dog," I reminded him.

"But you wouldn't have me," he pointed out, "or Luke or Min or Buster. See what you'd have missed."

"Yeah, I guess so," I said, but I was doubtful.

"Luke and Min are wonderful," Tex said. "Steady. You'll always have them."

"What do you mean, Tex?" I asked, suddenly suspicious. "What are you trying to tell me?"

"I've wanted to mention it the last few days," Tex apologized, "but I just haven't had a chance. Like I said, I've been here a long time, for me, and I have to be moving on again."

"Moving on?" I asked with a little shake of my head. "Why?" I had thought of him as someone like Luke or Min, someone who would stay.

"I have a chance to buy a little tavern in Newark, cheap," he said. "Mr. Neumann, the liquor salesman, told me about it. I've always wanted my own business, but this is the first one that's come along I could afford. It's in a crummy neighborhood, but I'll make something of it."

I felt the tears piling up in my eyes. "You're my best friend here," I said. "I don't want you to go."

"I'll miss you, Princess, you know I will," Tex explained, "but I can't let this opportunity pass me by. I've muffed too many opportunities in my life already."

"I didn't think you'd be like the others," I said. "I didn't think you'd be a fly-by-night."

"You still have Luke and Min," Tex said. "They were your good friends before I came, and they still are."

"They're not like you," I said. I was angry. "They're not really friends. They just sort of take care of me. I don't tell stories with them, or talk about things."

"Listen, Rosie," Tex said, taking my hand, "wherever I go, whatever I do, I'll still be your friend. Nothing can change that."

I shook my head. I didn't believe him. What good was a friend you never saw or talked to?

"Anyway," he went on, "I'm not going for almost a month. We have plenty of time to finish up the story we're working on."

"We've never finished a story yet," I said, pulling my hand out of his. "We always get tired of the one we're on, and we stop in the middle."

"Are you tired of this one?" Tex asked.

"No," I admitted. "This is a good one."

"Then let's get on with it," he said.

 *I*n a few moments Count Blackrose, his two soldiers, and Rosalie could no longer hear the shouts and screams of the Limbergers. The three horses were reined in, and the soldier carrying Rosalie bound her hands behind her back with a rope and placed a handkerchief in her mouth. Then they started off again, Rosalie now mounted behind the man, a rope around her waist connected to his.

Night fell. In spite of her fear, anger, and discomfort, Rosalie was finally overcome by the jogging motion and her exhaustion. She dozed off against the soldier's back. Time passed; Rosalie did not know how much. Suddenly she was shoved rudely awake, and half-carried, half-dragged through a door, down endless steps and passages, to a cell, into which, still bound and gagged, she was shoved unceremoniously. "Take care of her, jailer," said the soldier to a shaggy form huddled in a corner, and then he left.

The dungeon was dimly lit by a lantern set on the floor. Rosalie heard rats scuttling in the corners and saw heavy drops of white dampness on the rough-cut stone walls. The shaggy form in the corner lifted up its huge bulk and moved toward her. It was an incredibly tall form, so tall it had to hunch over in the low-ceilinged room, and it moved with a lumbering, heavy gait. Anyone else would have found its approach menacing, but Rosalie recognized it instantly. It moved toward her rapidly, for all its heaviness, and in a moment had removed the gag and her bonds.

"Old One," Rosalie cried, "you're here! Are you the jailer?"

"I am for tonight," the bear replied with a laugh. "Fortunately, the soldier was in too much of a hurry to notice, and the real jailer is in no condition to tell."

"Where is he?" Rosalie asked.

"Under the bed, drunk," the bear told her. "We'd better get out of here before he wakes up."

"Yes, we'd better," Rosalie agreed. "Though I'm not so sure you're as much my friend as I thought you were. Why didn't you make me leave the Limbergers when I still had the chance?"

"You have to make your own decisions," the Old One responded. "And now, I'm here, am I not? How do you know I did not intend all along to be here? How do you know that here is not where you're meant to be?"

"Why?" Rosalie protested. "Why would I be destined to end up in any place as horrid as this dungeon deep inside Count Blackrose's castle?"

"Not in the dungeon," the Old One explained in a tone that he might have employed in addressing a mentally underdeveloped four-year-old. "In Count Blackrose's castle, where your secret is—the secret of who you are."

"It's here?" Rosalie asked. "Here? Where? How do you know that?"

"Think, Rosalie, think," the Old One responded impatiently.

So Rosalie thought. "The paper," she said after a moment. "The paper is here. If it really had been full of gibberish, as Count Blackrose said it was, he would have torn it up. He wouldn't have folded it so carefully and put it in his pocket."

The bear nodded. "Now you're talking sense, Rosalie."

"But if the paper was in the Limbergers' cottage all the time, and if it really does hold the secret of my identity, why didn't you tell me about it? If you know so much, why didn't you tell me? Why did Count Blackrose have to come and kidnap me at all? Why did you let such a terrible thing happen to me?"

"What has to be has to be, Rosalie," the bear replied. "I'm here now, am I not? That will have to be good enough."

"What has to be has to be," Rosalie repeated, imitating the Old One's rich, honey-soaked voice. "I like it better when you talk regular," she went on in her own tones. "When you make these great big mysterious statements, I don't believe you. I think you're just trying to cover up your own mistakes."

119

"Everyone makes mistakes," the Old One said with a little sniff. "Including you!"

"Sure I make mistakes," Rosalie said. "I'm only eleven years old. My biggest mistake was opening the door to my tower and letting it slam shut behind me."

"Do you really think so?" the bear asked her.

Rosalie laughed ruefully and shook her head. "No," she said, "I really don't. Everything exactly the same day after day, that was pretty bad. Being in jail, that's the worst. But of course, if one must be in jail, one would naturally prefer my tower to this dungeon."

"Well, then let's get out of this dungeon right now," the Old One replied briskly. "Frankly, Blackrose did fool me there for a while. He acted a lot faster than I'd expected him to."

"The witch," Rosalie said. "What do you think the witch has to do with all of this? Who is she?"

The Old One's forehead wrinkled in a frown as he replied slowly, "A witch? It can only be Liederkranz. What do you know of her?"

"Blackrose mentioned a witch," Rosalie said, "a witch who was going to bleach out my freckles. Bleach out my life, more likely, I expect."

The Old One nodded. "I expect you're right," he agreed. As he spoke, a deep groan issued forth from under the cot. The jailer turned over, and an empty bottle rolled out of his hand and did not stop until it hit the wall on the other side of the room. "He's waking up," Rosalie said. "Whatever you put in his bottle must be wearing off. Let's get out of here."

The Old One picked up the jailer's keys, which he had removed from the man's belt before Rosalie's arrival. He unlocked the door to the cell and the two of them walked out into the passageway. Suddenly the Old One dropped down on all fours. "Get on my back, Rosalie," he said. "We'll move faster that way."

Rosalie was tired, and glad for the ride, but she did not believe that traveling on the bear's back would be fast, for whenever she had seen him move, he seemed to lumber along heavily and slowly. But that was perhaps because she had only seen him walking in an upright position, which he might have found unnatural, because once down on all fours, he seemed to glide along as quick as a bird, as smooth as a fish. His gait was still rolling and comfortable, yet before she had taken three breaths, they were outside the castle. Rosalie had no recollection whatsoever of passages or steps or doors. They were simply outside, surrounded by the cool, black night sky. There was no moon, only a thousand pinpoints of starlight to ease the darkness.

The two of them stood for a moment in the starlight, looking at each other. It was apparent

that neither of them knew quite what to do next. "It would be foolish to go inside the castle," the Old One said, breaking the silence suddenly, "until you have figured out some way of getting what you want to know out of Blackrose without giving him the opportunity to slap you back into that dungeon."

"Or worse," Rosalie added grimly. "I think we should go see the witch."

"Liederkranz? But she's on his side," the Old One replied. "She works for him."

"But she won't know that I don't," Rosalie said. "She won't know who I am."

"I wouldn't bet on that," the bear said with a shake of his shaggy head. "She certainly knows who I am." But then he added, "It's worth a try. Liederkranz can be dealt with."

Rosalie heaved a huge sigh. "All of this is so difficult," she said. "I don't know anything. I don't know what it's all about. I feel as if I were groping about in the dark, without even the smallest candle or tiniest star to light the way."

The bear patted her on the shoulder with his huge paw. "Come on, Rosalie," he said, "let's find Liederkranz. I've handled her before; I daresay I can do it again."

The little village huddled inside the castle walls consisted of perhaps fifteen hovels altogether. Rosalie knocked at the very nearest one. A young woman holding a baby opened the door a crack and peered out suspiciously. "Well," she asked, "what is it? What do you want?"

The Old One stood off in the shadows and let Rosalie do the talking in order to avoid complicated explanations concerning the presence of a very large talking bear in Count Blackrose's courtyard. "I'm looking for the witch," Rosalie said. "Can you tell me which is her cottage?"

"What would you want with her?" the woman asked crossly. "You're too young to be after a love potion."

"What about hate potions?" Rosalie asked. "I'm not too young for them, am I?"

"You got money?" the young woman asked.

"What business is that of yours?" Rosalie rejoined sharply. "It's the witch I've come to talk with."

"Well, aren't we the hoity-toity one!" the woman said with a sneer. "I'll have you know the witch is my mother, and I won't have her wasting any more of her time on people who have no money. I wish I'd inherited her powers. If I had, I'd show her how to turn them to good account."

"Let her in," a voice called from inside the cottage. "Come along, Jarlsberg, and let her in. I've been waiting for her all evening."

"Oh, all right, Mother," Jarlsberg said grudgingly as she threw open the door.

Rosalie turned and beckoned to the Old One. The woman let out a screech as he walked through the door, but the voice inside the cottage called out, "Don't be childish, Jarlsberg. It's only a bear. Haven't you ever seen a bear before? I've been expecting him too." Rosalie and the Old One walked across the room to a narrow bed which was set against the wall. It was covered with a tattered quilt and in it lay a woman who was not so much old as pale, ill, and tired-looking.

"Are you really the witch?" Rosalie asked disbelievingly.

"Yes," said the woman in the bed, "I am. Do you find that idea so hard to swallow?"

"If you have magic powers, why don't you use them to take better care of yourself?" Rosalie asked.

"A witch can't do everything," she replied. "Only some things."

"Like the Old One," Rosalie said.

"The powers of all of us are limited," the witch replied. "I am like most other witches. I can do no good for myself; only evil to others."

"Why, that's terrible," Rosalie said in a voice full of the shock and pity she felt.

"Yes," the witch agreed calmly. "A witch's lot is not a happy one. I am dependent on unpleasant types like Count Blackrose for my living. It's only people like him who have any use for my abilities."

"But your daughter said something about love potions," Rosalie recalled.

"Love potions? Humph!" the witch snorted. "They're the worst of all."

"You mean they don't work?" Rosalie asked.

"They work all too well," the witch said. "You tell her, Old One. You know all about it."

"It's a long story," the Old One said with a sigh, "much too long a story to tell now. But Liederkranz is right. Using a love potion to make someone love you who doesn't want to love you never did anyone any good at all." The bear came closer to the old woman's bed and looked at her for a long moment. "You used to live in the Floribunda Forest," he said. "When did you come here?"

"Blackrose brought me here," Liederkranz replied, "and not so long ago, either. He said he had a special job for me that I could only do here, at the castle. However, since I've come, he hasn't called on me for anything big. One young woman was so foolish as to spurn the Count's favors. I gave her a few good stomach cramps, and made some warts pop up on her lover's face." Here Liederkranz paused and heaved a huge sigh. "Ai-eee, the foolish things I have to stoop to."

"Then why do you do them?" Rosalie asked.

The old woman shrugged. "We have to make a living with whatever gifts nature blessed us," she replied. "We have to eat."

"Eat?" the daughter snorted. She had stood close to them all the while, rocking her fretful baby in her arms and listening to what they were saying. "Count Blackrose has given us nothing but moldy black bread and weak tea since we got here. So much for all of his fine promises."

"The other people in the neighborhood have seen to it that we haven't lacked for fresh meat, good cheese, beer, and barley cake," the witch replied. She turned to Rosalie. "Don't mind Jarlsberg," she said apologetically. "She's a chronic complainer, and terribly jealous of me. She wishes she were a witch too. She doesn't know how lucky she is. Listen, Jarlsberg," she addressed her daughter again, "you know the Count brought us here for a big job. When it's done, he'll reward us suitably, if he knows what's good for him."

"How long do we have to wait?" Jarlsberg whined. "This climate is terrible for the baby. He hasn't stopped crying since we got here."

"He never did anything but cry before we came here, either. Anyway, we won't have to wait much longer," Liederkranz continued soothingly. "Not long at all. The time is fast approaching. I feel it in my bones." She smiled and winked knowingly

126

at Rosalie, who felt a shudder pass through her whole body.

"You don't like the Count much, do you?" Rosalie commented.

"I hate him, my darling," the witch replied. "He's not to be trusted."

"But you can trust us," Rosalie said. "You can trust the Old One and me. You can tell that, can't you?"

"Certainly, my darling," the witch agreed.

"So you wouldn't hurt us, if the Count asked you to, would you?" Rosalie asked.

"Of course I would, my darling," the witch replied in apparent surprise. "I explained all that to you. I have to practice my profession. What else am I supposed to do?"

"This is what you're supposed to do," the Old One said. He sat down on the edge of the witch's bed. It creaked with his weight, but it didn't collapse. The Old One held out his paw to her. Rosalie could see something gleaming in it. It gleamed so brightly that it seemed to light up the whole side of the cottage. Rosalie stepped closer and saw that it was a great golden key, a key exactly like the one with which she had opened her tower door. Perhaps it was the very same one. Rosalie wondered if the Voice had given it to the Old One. She hoped so. That would mean that even though her Voice had not been able to come to

127

her during all those long weeks at the Limbergers', it had not forgotten about her entirely.

The witch reached out her bony hand to grab the key, but the Old One, whose quickness never ceased to surprise Rosalie, closed his great paw over it. "It's what you want," the Old One said. "I know it."

"It's what Count Blackrose promised me," the witch whispered, her glittering eyes still staring at the Old One's paw, even though the key was now completely hidden. "He promised it to me long ago."

"But as you can see," the Old One said, "it's not his to dispose of, not anymore. It's mine. So now you will do what I say, and then the key that opens every lock in the world will be yours. As Rosalie said, you can trust us."

"I know, I know," the witch replied with an impatient wave of her hand, "but you know too that I can do no good. Only evil. So what is there that I can do for you?"

"You can refrain from doing evil, at least to us," the Old One said. "That's all. No matter what Count Blackrose asks you to do to us, you will not do it. And if any of his soldiers, or he himself, tries to harm us, you will strike them dead on the spot."

"Agreed, agreed," the witch said, her mouth

128

watering at the mere idea of the key. "Now give it to me. Give it to me."

"Don't be ridiculous," the Old One said. "You'll wait until we're safely out of here, with Rosalie knowing what it is she wants to know. You can trust us, but we can't trust you!"

The witch laughed humorlessly. "True enough," she admitted. "Jarlsberg," she ordered, "help me out of this bed. Help me to dress."

Jarlsberg shoved the baby at Rosalie. "Here," she muttered, "you see if you have any better luck with him than I do." Rosalie looked at the baby. He was certainly the skinniest, ugliest creature she'd ever seen, looking much more like a plucked chicken than a human being. But he was very strong, and when Rosalie held out her finger to him, he grabbed it with a grip of iron and reduced his mighty cries to occasional fretful sobs. Rosalie felt as if he would pull her finger right out of its socket, but she let him hold on to it since it seemed to comfort him, and anything was better than his screams. Meanwhile, Jarlsberg helped the old woman up, and assisted her in putting on a soiled and tattered dress over her nightgown. "Don't you have anything cleaner?" the Old One asked. Rosalie was not surprised. She knew he put a high value on a good appearance. "After all," the bear continued, "we are

129

going to see Count Blackrose. He is a member of the aristocracy, and no matter how wicked a nobleman is, one ought to show him a certain degree of respect."

"This is the best we have," Jarlsberg replied shortly. "It will have to do. We're not millionaires, you know."

"You're misers is what you are," the Old One said disdainfully. "You've got the greatest cache of gold in the universe hidden away in the Floribunda Forest. You just don't want to spend it."

"How do you know that?" The witch almost spit the words at him in her fury. "Did you steal it?"

"Of course not," the Old One replied, letting his anger show in his voice. "Do you think that I only do evil, like a witch? I can do what I can do, and there isn't much that lies under the ground that I don't know about. That's how I found the golden key. The Count made the mistake of burying it."

"Let's get on with our business, then," Liederkranz announced firmly. She straightened up and hurried toward the door. Her illness was in the same class as her poverty—phony. She certainly seemed a lot stronger than she had when Rosalie and the Old One had first come in. "The sooner I can add that gold key to my precious hoard," she said, "the happier I'll be. And the sooner I'm shook of you two, the safer I'll be!"

She walked briskly out the cottage door. Rosalie and the Old One followed her into the castle courtyard.

What's in a name?
that which we call a rose
By any other name
would smell as sweet . . .

Shakespeare said that. It was another one of the rose verses Rachel was collecting for me. After she showed it to me, I thought about it a lot. I decided I didn't believe it. A rose might smell as sweet if it had another name, but it wouldn't be a rose. It would be something else. And if I didn't have a funny old name like Rose, I'd have been someone else. If Estelle Coviella had a different name, she would have turned out to be a different kind of person. A name that sounds like music may help you to be happy. Estelle Coviella was certainly happy.

132

Mom gave me a dollar to buy Estelle a birthday present. I added a quarter of my own because she deserved something really good. Wednesday, after school, I walked downtown to get it. Instead of one big thing, I decided to buy her many little things, wrap each one separately, and then put them all in a big box which I would also wrap. That way she could have a lot of extra fun opening a lot of extra presents.

I went into Woolworth's and picked out two sets of paper dolls, bride paper dolls and Junior Miss paper dools. We had all seen the movie *Junior Miss,* with Peggy Ann Garner, and we had all loved it. I mean, all the girls in my class had loved it. Rachel had liked it too. Dan had thought it was silly. He only liked John Wayne and Gary Cooper and people like that. Of course, he went to the movies every Saturday afternoon anyway, just like the rest of us, no matter what was playing. But this coming Saturday I wouldn't be going. I'd be going to Estelle Coviella's birthday party.

Also in Woolworth's I bought a box of note paper, a set of really good jacks that came with two balls, a box of crayons, a package of drawing paper, two pencils, two pens, and a lipstick. The lipstick was just for laughs. Luckily, I didn't have to waste any of the money on wrapping paper. Whenever Mom got a present, she unwrapped it very, very carefully, and saved the paper so that one of us could use it again. She made us do the same, at least when she was watching. I did it even when she wasn't watching, but it was hard for Rachel and Dan to unwrap things neatly.

I waited for Mom in front of Stein's Drugstore on the corner of Main and Mill Race Streets. Mom had her hair done every Wednesday afternoon. We had arranged that she would pick me up at the corner when we were both finished. I knew she'd be late. She was always late. Whenever she tried to get out of the Inn, something came up to delay her. She had to answer the phone or talk to a customer, or solve a problem for one of the help. That meant that she never made it to the beauty parlor at the time she was supposed to, and so, of course, she never got out on time either. But I was used to that. I didn't really expect her to show up at four-fifteen, like she'd said she would, but I was standing in front of Stein's on the dot. If by some chance she should make it when she was supposed to, and I wasn't there, she'd be furious. She thought it was all right for us to wait for her, but she got mad if she ever had to wait for us.

So I waited. I waited and waited. I waited until the clock hanging outside the bank across the street said five o'clock. It was getting dark, and I began to think about walking home. Maybe she'd forgotten she was supposed to pick me up. But if I started walking, and she came, and I wasn't there, she'd really eat me up. I could go into the drugstore and phone the Inn, but I didn't have a nickel, and besides, I might miss her that way too.

I was still wondering what I ought to do, when her

old Pontiac station wagon pulled up to the curb at last. "What happened, Mom?" I asked as I climbed into the car. "I was beginning to get worried."

"I'm sorry, darling, really I am," she replied. "If there was some way to phone you, I would have. But there was just no way. Buster had some kind of attack. Mrs. Dunleigh got hysterical and the Major was in the city, so I had to rush the dog to the vet for a shot. *I* had to do it. As if I don't have enough to do. I should never have let them stay at the Inn with a dog. Never."

"How's Buster now?" I asked. I was worried about him.

"Oh, he's all right," Mom said. "The shot seemed to fix him up immediately. I brought him right back home."

"Did Mrs. Dunleigh go to the vet with you?"

"She wanted to," Mom said, "but I wouldn't let her. That's all I needed, an hysterical woman in the car with me. I can't stand people like Mrs. Dunleigh, people with no self-control. I can't stand them."

"She seems very self-controlled to me," I said. "She never talks above a whisper."

"She's weak," Mom said, "and silly. I can't abide weak, silly people. Imagine, getting so worked up over a dog."

"She has no children," I tried to explain, "and the Major is always so busy."

"Oh, I guess she has reasons," Mom said, "but I still can't stand her. I only let Buster stay because the Major was willing to pay the weekly rate for the best room in

135

the Inn, even though they're staying for months. I couldn't turn that down. They eat almost all their meals at the Inn, too, at the regular menu prices, so I guess I can afford to rush that stupid dog to the vet if I have to. But I was worried about my appointment at the beauty parlor, and then at the beauty parlor I was worried about you."

"Well, that's all right," I said. "I don't mind, now that I know why. You couldn't just let Buster die."

"I guess you're right," Mom said. "I guess I couldn't."

But Buster did die. He died late Saturday morning. I was in my room, dressing for Estelle's party. Mom had told me if I was all ready before the wedding reception came in, she'd have time to braid my hair properly, and then I could walk to Estelle's house. I could walk it easily. I had to cross the highway to get there, but after that it was in a different direction from school, and not as far.

Suddenly I heard a ghastly shriek. Then I heard another one. I had never heard anything like them in all my life, except in a Frankenstein movie. I ran out into the hall. Olga, the chambermaid, came out in the hall too, from Room #9 where she was cleaning. "Olga, what happened?" I asked.

Her little brown eyes opened as wide as they could. "Must be Mrs. Dunleigh," she whispered. "Everybody else gone; all other rooms empty." The Major wasn't home either. I had seen him in the lobby, early in the morning, on his way to the city again. For a man who was retired, he had an awful lot of business in the city if he even had to go in on a Saturday.

There were no more shrieks, but when I knocked on the door of Room #17, I could hear Mrs. Dunleigh sobbing. She didn't answer my knock. I tried the door, but it was locked. Olga was standing right behind me, her face expressionless. "Olga," I said, "open the door with the passkey."

"No, Rosie, I don't think so. Mrs. Dunleigh, she be mad, we open door."

"Olga, open the door," I insisted. "We can't just leave her in there hysterical, all by herself."

Olga handed me the passkey. "You open door," she said. "Let it be on your head."

I opened the door. Mrs. Dunleigh was kneeling by her bed. Buster lay at the foot of the bed, and her arms were thrown across him. Tears streamed down her face, streaking her white powder. I ran over to her and put my hand on her shoulder. "Mrs. Dunleigh," I said, "what's the matter?" She didn't answer me; she only lifted her hand and let it drop again on Buster.

I looked at the dog. His body lay rigid and stiff. His open, staring eyes did not move. I touched him too, and drew my hand back as soon as I felt his cold, clammy skin. He was dead. Buster was dead.

A shudder shot through my whole body, and then my hands began to tremble. I could feel the tears form in my eyes, and for a minute I just stood there, letting them roll down my cheeks. Mrs. Dunleigh was sobbing out loud. I couldn't see her face anymore because she had buried it in the bedclothes, but I could see her shoulders shaking. She was making so much noise she sounded as if she was choking to death herself.

I took a Kleenex out of the box on the night table, wiped my face, and blew my nose. I put my hand on Mrs. Dunleigh's shoulder again. "It's all right, Mrs. Dunleigh," I said. "It's all right." I knew it wasn't all right, but I didn't know what else to say.

Mrs. Dunleigh went right on sobbing. She didn't say anything. She just kept crying and crying. I didn't know what to do. She certainly wasn't paying any attention to me, but I was afraid to leave her. I couldn't leave her, not hysterical like that, her hand clutching and unclutching the loose skin around poor Buster's neck. I stood there, with my hand on her shoulder, trying to keep back my own tears. Two of us hysterical would have been too much.

It seemed to me that a long time passed and I didn't move. Mrs. Dunleigh didn't change her position either, but her body continued to shake with her sobs. I glanced over at the clock on the night table. It was quarter of twelve already. The party began at noon, and I was supposed to walk over. The walk would take me nearly half an hour, and my hair wasn't even braided yet.

Suddenly Mrs. Dunleigh let out another ear-piercing screech, and this time her hand did not let go of Buster's neck. I reached out and one by one straightened out her clutching fingers. Then I slipped a pillow out of its Con-

138

solidated Laundry pillowcase. My father had died six years before. I didn't really remember him. He had been in bed most of the time for a year before he died. I had hardly ever seen him. However, I remembered his funeral. Everyone had cried a lot, but they seemed to feel better afterwards, at least for a little while.

"Look, Mrs. Dunleigh," I said, "you know what we're going to do? We're going to have a proper funeral for Buster. Let's wrap him in this pillowcase and carry him downstairs and bury him in the field out back. And then we'll mark where we bury him with a nice white rock."

Mrs. Dunleigh seemed to hear me. She looked up at me and nodded. "That's a good idea," she said in a whisper so low I could barely make out her words. She went into the bathroom and washed and repowdered her face. By the time she came out again, I had Buster neatly wrapped inside the pillowcase. When she saw the little bundle lying on the floor, I thought she was going to start shrieking again. I was a little annoyed. I had done the hard part.

"What happened?" I asked quickly. "How did he die?" I thought that if she were talking, she wouldn't be able to shriek.

"He seemed fine," Mrs. Dunleigh managed to tell me, softly and slowly. "Of course, he had trouble breathing, but that's been the case for more than a year now. The vet gave him that shot Wednesday, and he really seemed all right."

We walked out into the hall together. I was carrying
Buster. Mrs. Dunleigh kept right on talking. I had to
strain my ears to hear her, but at least she seemed
calmer. "This morning he was no different than he had
been last night. After the Major left, he had his breakfast while I had mine." Since the Inn didn't serve
breakfast, the Dunleighs kept an electric coffeepot and
some fruit in their room. "Then I went into the bathroom to get dressed," she continued. "I never liked to
get dressed in front of Buster. It didn't seem right to
me, though I know some people would think that was
foolish. But since he had that attack on Wednesday,
I should have known better than to leave him alone.
I should have known better. If I had been with him,
perhaps I could have saved him."

She looked as if she were about to sob again, so I
said very quickly, "How could you have saved him?
I'm sure he just died, and he would have done that
whether you had been in the room or not. What happened when you came back?"

"Buster was lying on the bed right where I'd left
him, so I didn't think anything of it at all, until I went
over there. Then I saw he was stiff and his eyes were
staring, and I realized he was dead. He died without
making a single sound."

"He was a brave dog," I said, "a brave dog and a
good dog."

In the lobby we met my mother, hurrying toward
us from the Holiday Room. Olga was right behind her.

140

"What's the matter, Mrs. Dunleigh?" she asked. "Olga told me you weren't feeling well."

"Buster died," I explained. "We're going to bury him now."

"Bury him?" My mother raised her eyebrows. "I could just take him to the vet later, after the wedding reception. The vet would dispose of him. It would be easier."

"Dispose of him?" Mrs. Dunleigh whispered. Her mouth hung open, and her eyes grew wide. If Mom started Mrs. Dunleigh screaming again, I'd really be furious.

"Mrs. Dunleigh likes the idea of a funeral," I said. "When I told her about it, she stopped crying."

"Rosie said it would be all right," Mrs. Dunleigh said in an almost normal tone of voice. "She said it would be all right to bury Buster in the back field behind the Inn."

Mom realized she'd made a mistake. "Of course it's all right," she said. "It's a wonderful idea. You go right ahead. Rosie will help you."

"Would you like to come?" Mrs. Dunleigh asked. "I don't think I know any prayers for the dead. It's so long since I've been to a funeral. We don't even go to church. Maybe you know a Jewish prayer. I don't think Buster would mind if we said a Jewish prayer."

"I'd like to come," Mom said. "I really would. Thanks for asking me. But I can't. We're so busy this afternoon. Rosie will take care of everything. I have an extra Bible in the office. The Gideons left it when they were putting them in all the rooms. You can take it outside with you and Rosie can read the Twenty-third Psalm. That goes well at any funeral, no matter what the religion." She hurried into the office and got the Bible for us. Then she rushed away toward the bar.

I got a spade from the garage. Fortunately, it had rained the night before and it was not at all cold for December. The ground was soft and I was able to dig a hole deep enough for little Buster. He had never been a large dog, and he seemed to have shrunk up quite a bit since I'd first known him. Mrs. Dunleigh just stood there and watched me. It was hard work. If Sylvester hadn't been so busy, I'd have gotten him to help me, but he was in the kitchen, washing dishes. Everyone at the Inn was busy, even Rachel, who was minding the checkroom. The only one who wasn't busy was Dan, but he was over at Gary's or Bruce's house. He went to one of them every Saturday before the movies to play baseball or football, depending on the season.

So I dug the hole myself. When I thought it was deep enough, I asked Mrs. Dunleigh if she cared to place Buster's body in the grave. She shook her head, so I picked up the bundle myself and laid it in the shallow hole. Then I took the Bible from Mrs. Dunleigh's limp hand and read "The Lord is My Shepherd." It didn't seem like enough, but I didn't know what else to do. The nearest synagogue was in Plainfield, and we only went there on Rosh Hashanah and Yom Kippur, so I didn't really know much. "How about a hymn, Mrs. Dunleigh?" I asked. "Maybe you know a hymn you could sing."

She stared at me for a moment, and then, without saying a word, she opened her mouth and a tune came out.

> Abide with me; fast falls the eventide;
> The darkness deepens; Lord, with me abide;
> When other helpers fail, and comforts flee,
> Help of the helpless, O abide with me.

It was the right hymn. When the song was done, I handed Mrs. Dunleigh the shovel. She was able to throw a little dirt into the grave. I finished the job, and then I went around to the front of the building. There was a flagpole in the center of a grass circle in the middle of our long drive, and the flagpole was surrounded by whitewashed rocks. They were heavy, but I managed to lug one of them around to the back and place it on Buster's grave. "This way, you'll always know where it is," I told Mrs. Dunleigh. "I dug the grave here, under this tree, so the mower won't disturb the stone when Sylvester cuts the grass in the summertime."

After we put the marker on the grave, we walked back around to the front of the building. We went into the lobby. The clock above the registration desk told me it was quarter of one. I was filthy from all that digging and I would have to bathe and change before I went to the party. I really didn't have another good dress. I'd have to wear my gray skirt and blue sweater again, and manage my hair as best I could. I certainly had missed lunch, but maybe I could get to Estelle's in time for cake and ice cream.

I walked up the stairs with Mrs. Dunleigh. When we got to my room, I stopped by the door. "Goodbye, Mrs. Dunleigh," I said. "I'm really sorry about Buster. I hope you feel better soon."

"Where are you going, Rosie?" Mrs. Dunleigh asked me, her hand clutching my arm as tightly as it had clung to Buster's body. "I thought you would come back to my room with me."

"I can't, Mrs. Dunleigh," I tried to explain. "I have to get cleaned up. I'm going to a birthday party."

"Don't leave me alone, Rosie," Mrs. Dunleigh whispered desperately. "Please don't leave me alone. I don't know what I'll do if I'm alone today."

"You wouldn't start screeching again, would you, Mrs. Dunleigh?" I asked.

"I might," she replied with a sigh. "Who knows?"

"The Major will be back soon," I said as cheerfully as I could. "There can't be much business for him to take care of in the city on Saturday. Besides, you're not really alone here. There are hundreds of people in the building."

"The Major won't be back until dinner. I need someone with me, next to me—someone who understands about Buster. Please, Rosie, please stay with me. Just because there are a lot of other people around doesn't mean I'm not alone!"

No one knew that better than I. So I stayed with her. She came with me into my room while I washed up and changed. After that, she wanted to go sit in her room, but that was too much for me. I made her come down into the lobby, where we could at least watch the people at the wedding. I called Estelle from the phone in my mother's office. "Cripes, Rosie," she said when her mother got her to the phone, "where are you? I thought you'd forgotten."

Not likely. "Look," I said, "I can't come. I'm really sorry, because I really wanted to come in the worst way, but there's this lady at the Inn, and she had this dog—"

"Oh, that's too bad," Estelle interrupted. "We're having a lot of fun. I can't stop to talk now. We're right in the middle of a game of Spin-the-bottle. I had to kiss Bart Flint. Ugh!"

"You mean there are boys there?" I asked. I almost fainted when I heard that.

"Sure," Estelle said. "Didn't I tell you?"

"No," I said.

"Well, I gotta go. You'll tell me everything Monday, and I'll tell you. Bye." And without another word, she hung up.

There were boys at the party! I hadn't even known.

But if I had known, would it have made any difference? I couldn't have gone anyway. There was just no way, no way at all, that I could have left Mrs. Dunleigh.

I went back to her and we sat together for the rest of that whole endless afternoon. I let her cry every now and then, but when it looked like she was going to get hysterical again, or scream, I started to talk about something—about some cute trick of Buster's or about some of the people in the lobby, or even about some of the kids at school. I talked about anything at all, just to distract her from her own misery. I was so busy keeping her occupied, I had no chance to cry over Buster myself!

Mom walked back and forth through the lobby a few times, but she never saw us. We were over in a corner by the fireplace, and there were always other people around. Mom didn't look to the right or the left when she was rushing from one place to another. After a while I realized I was hungry. I got us some sandwiches and tea from Pedro at three o'clock. Mrs. Dunleigh just sipped a little of the tea so I ate her sandwich too.

About five o'clock I saw the Major come through the lobby. I was never so happy to lay eyes on a person in my life. I jumped up and ran toward him. "Major," I whispered, "I have something to tell you." Mrs. Dunleigh had gotten up out of her chair. She didn't come across the room to join us, but stood there, watching us. "Buster is dead," I said. "He died this morning."

"Well," the Major said, "it's about time. I told Mrs. Dunleigh a thousand times she ought to have him put out of his misery."

"She's taking it very hard," I said. "I had to sit with her all afternoon. She wouldn't let me leave her."

"That was kind of you, Rosie," Major Dunleigh said. "Very kind of you." He reached in his pocket and pulled out a wad of bills. He peeled off a single and held it out to me. "Here, please, take this for your trouble."

"I don't want any money, Major Dunleigh," I said. "That's not why I did it."

"Of course not," he said. I could tell from the tone of his voice that he didn't really believe me. "But take it anyway."

"No," I replied angrily, "I won't. You just go take care of Mrs. Dunleigh now. That's all I want." I did not go back over to her. I just turned and called out, "So long, Mrs. Dunleigh. I'll see you later." I left them both and walked into the bar as quickly as I could without actually running.

Mother was in the bar, talking to Tex about the banquet that was coming in after the wedding reception went out, and about the regular Saturday night business. It was only a couple of weeks until Christmas, and the Inn was very busy. There was more business in one week in December than there was in the whole month of January put together.

"Oh, darling," Mom said when she saw me, "back from your party already?"

"I'm sure the party's over by now," I said. "It's after five. It started at noon."

"Was it fun?" Mom asked.

"I didn't go."

"You didn't go!" For once I'd said something that really surprised her. "But you were looking forward to it so much. Why on earth didn't you go?"

"I had to stay with Mrs. Dunleigh. I couldn't leave her alone. She wouldn't let me leave her alone, and I couldn't do it anyway. She was too upset. I don't know what she would have done if someone hadn't stayed with her."

"Why, that miserable, silly little woman," Mom said, "spoiling your afternoon that way. I wish I'd known."

"What could you have done?" I asked. "Someone had to stay with her. No one else around here could have. Everyone else was too busy. She didn't want anyone else anyway. No one else understood."

My mother looked at me for a long moment. Then she leaned over and kissed me on the cheek. "What was that for?" I asked.

"We'll talk about it later," she said. "When I'm not so busy." She hurried away, and I climbed up on one of the bar stools. It was quiet in the bar between parties. While he cleaned up, Tex and I talked about Rosalie and the great bear and the Land of Three Roses. It was a good thing. It kept me from thinking too much about the party I'd missed, or about poor Buster. Later on, in bed, I could cry for him.

*T*he witch Liederkranz led the way across the castle courtyard, followed by the bear. Rosalie trailed behind, though she walked as quickly as she could to keep up with the long strides of the two in front of her. When they got to the great iron gate which opened into the castle tower itself, the witch said to the guard, "Tell Count Blackrose the witch Liederkranz has come to see him."

"The Count will see no one this evening," the guard replied through pursed lips, "least of all the likes of you."

"Tell him Rosalie comes with me," the witch added sharply. "You can be sure that if Count Blackrose ever finds out you denied Rosalie entrance, your life won't be worth the boots you're standing in. You know me well enough, Sergeant Boursin, to know that I don't make idle threats."

Sergeant Boursin stared directly into Liederkranz's eyes. She returned his stare without flinching. Abruptly he turned and called through the iron gate, "Captain Larosa, Captain Larosa."

Footsteps echoed across a stone floor, and in a moment a tall figure in the black uniform trimmed in rose and gold that Rosalie had seen earlier stood on the other side of the gate. "What is it, Sergeant?" he asked briskly.

"The witch says she's brought someone to see Count Blackrose—someone named Rosalie, whoever she is. What should I do?" the sergeant queried.

"I'll find out," Captain Larosa replied. "With a name like Rosalie, the Count may well want to see her. She comes with the witch, so we can't be too careful."

Captain Larosa disappeared again into the dimness. The witch, the bear, and Rosalie stood silently in the chill air waiting for his return. Rosalie huddled next to the Old One for warmth, and felt the safety of his great, hairy arm around her shoulders.

Captain Larosa was gone for what seemed an interminable length of time, but he returned at last and opened the gate for them himself. "Blackrose will see you," he said. He led them through the guardroom, down long corridors and through great, barren, drafty halls. Their journey was so endless that it was hard for Rosalie to believe they were in the same castle she and the bear had sped through like the wind just a few hours before. Soldiers in black uniforms lined the walls every step of the way.

They came at last to an apartment which was

much more comfortable than the others they had passed through. It was smaller and hung with rich, warm tapestries. A huge fire crackled in the hearth, for though it was summer, the night was chilly, and the castle damp. Blackrose was seated at a writing desk, with two guards at attention on either side and two more at each of the four entrances into the room. As they marched through the largest of the doors, one of the guards intoned, "The child Rosalie, the Old One, and the witch Liederkranz." Immediately Count Blackrose stood up and crossed the room, meeting them in the middle, before the blazing fire.

"Well, well, my dear," said Count Blackrose, "I'm sorry you weren't satisfied with my hospitality before. I'm glad indeed that you have experienced a change of heart and have decided to return. Of course, this time I think you will find your accommodations much more to your liking."

"I'm not planning to stay," Rosalie replied sharply. "Don't think it for a minute! You knew all along who I was, and you know a lot more about me than my name. I think it's time you told me who my mother and father are, and why I was shut in a tower all those years."

"Rosalie, my dear, what makes you think I know the answers to hard questions like that?" the Count said with a grim little smile.

"The paper," Rosalie said. "The paper the Limbergers gave you."

"A worthless piece of trash," Count Blackrose replied with a wave of his hand. "It means nothing."

"Then why didn't you tear it up?" Rosalie insisted.

"Oh, I have, you may be sure," the Count replied smoothly. "But naturally, I didn't do it on the spot. I had to read it carefully first. It's never wise to act too hastily."

"Well, then, Count Blackrose," Rosalie said, opening her blue eyes as wide as she could and lifting her chin, "we have nothing more to say to each other. I will leave you now." And she turned her back to him as if she were about to depart.

"Guards!" Blackrose's command rang out sharply. Immediately the soldiers by each of the entrances crossed their spears over the doorways. The count put his hand on Rosalie's shoulder and turned her around toward him. Her skin crawled beneath his touch, and she swept his hand from her shoulder as if it were a spider. "I'm afraid, darling Rosalie," the Count said in a silky voice, "that I must insist on your acceptance of my hospitality. The Old One must leave, of course, but the witch will stay with you. She'll keep you com-

152

pany. She'll see that no harm comes to you." He smiled broadly this time, revealing his large, sharp yellow teeth. "Won't you, my dear Liederkranz? Won't you stay with our darling Rosalie and see that she remains safe within the castle walls? We certainly don't want more unexpected departures like the one we experienced earlier this evening, do we?"

Rosalie glanced anxiously at the witch. She knew that Liederkranz had promised the Old One to do her no harm, but she didn't trust the witch any farther than she could throw her. All the Count had to do to get her back on his side was offer her something more valuable than the golden key. Hopefully, there *was* nothing more valuable.

Then the Old One spoke. "Excuse me, Count Blackrose," he said with elaborate courtesy, "but this conversation is absurd, and you know that as well as anyone else." He dropped from his upright stance to all fours. "You can't keep Rosalie here if I choose otherwise. Come, Rosalie," he ordered, "get on my back again, the way you did earlier." Rosalie was only too glad to obey. She leaped on his back with an ease that surprised even herself.

"Guards!" Blackrose screamed. All ten of the soldiers in the room stepped forward, and with

lowered spears pointed right at Rosalie and the Old One, they stood in a circle around the four in the middle of the room.

"Come, come, Blackrose," the Old One said softly, "what's a circle of spears to one who moves like the wind? They can do me no harm, nor Rosalie either, so long as she's on my back."

Count Blackrose's face flushed a deep, dark red. "Is that true, Liederkranz?" he asked the witch hoarsely.

"Yes, Count, it is," the witch replied. "The Old One and the wind are brothers."

"Well, do something about it," the Count urged. "You're related to all kinds of things too, aren't you? Do something about it. Rosalie can't be allowed to get away again. Twice in my life she escaped me, and you can be sure I won't stand around and let it happen a third time."

"What can you do about it?" Liederkranz asked with a shrug. "I won't stop them. The Old One promised me the golden key if I do them no harm. You promised it to me too, and you didn't even have it!"

"Help me," Count Blackrose insisted. "Help me or the spears of my soldiers will strike you down—here, this minute, on the spot."

The soldiers moved their spears forward in a threatening gesture, but the witch only laughed a dry humorless cackle. "My dear Count," she

154

said, "what can spears do to one who is sister of the night?"

"Count Blackrose," the Old One announced, his deep, honeyed voice filling all the corners of the room, "you can do nothing to us. Face the truth. You're beaten. Rosalie has escaped you."

Before Rosalie's very eyes, the Count seemed to shrink and grow old. His shoulders hunched, his hands hung limp at his side, and he shook his head slowly, as if it were torture to move. "So, you have beaten me, have you? Beaten me. Well, well, well . . ." His voice trailed off, and for a moment there was no sound in the room but the crackling of the logs in the fireplace. Then, suddenly, Count Blackrose straightened his shoulders and lifted his head. When he spoke again, his voice was as strong and as dangerous as it had ever been. "Well, well, well," he repeated briskly, "it's the first time anyone's beaten me, and I daresay it's the last. Our story isn't over yet, Rosalie, not by a long shot. We'll meet again, you can be sure, and let's see who comes out the winner next time. You can't cling to the Old One's coat forever, you know."

"I know," Rosalie said. "I don't want to. I'm not afraid."

"We'll see about that. At least I had the sense to leave two men at the Limbergers' cottage. If I don't send word by carrier pigeon before dawn, the Limbergers will hang from the oak tree in their yard at first light."

"The Limbergers? The Limbergers?" Rosalie asked. She climbed slowly off the Old One's back, though her hand still clutched at the fur of his neck. "Why the Limbergers? Why are you going to kill them?"

"It'll just make me feel a little better," Count Blackrose explained.

"I understand perfectly," Liederkranz commented.

"I would have killed them anyway," the Count said. "The only thing that might have stopped me was the discovery that they could in some way still be useful to me. But I have made no such discovery, so at dawn they die. They disobeyed my orders. They harbored a freckled child. They should have known better. In my domain, my word takes precedence over any message from the court at Rosehilde."

"That was their crime?" Rosalie said. "Letting me stay at their cottage was a crime? They are going to die because of me? All of them?"

"All of them," the Count said with a smile that showed all of his teeth.

"Odora too?"

"Odora too," the Count insisted, "if the branch of the oak tree will hold her. If it doesn't, one of my men will just run his sword through her. Peasants are supposed to hang. Only the nobility are privileged to die by the sword. But there are cases when exceptions have to be made."

"Odora is so young," Rosalie said, "and so foolish. It isn't fair."

"Oh, Rosalie, what difference does it make?" the Old One interrupted. "Come on, we've got to get out of here. We can't worry about them. They were awful people. They were terrible to you. They deserve whatever happens to them. That old man was the worst—poaching in my pool." Rosalie noticed that the bear spoke of the Limbergers as if they were already dead.

Rosalie let go of the bear's fur and took two steps toward Count Blackrose. "You said that if it was to your advantage, you would not kill them," she said to him. "Isn't that true?"

"Yes, Rosalie," Count Blackrose said softly. "That is true."

"Well, then," Rosalie said firmly, "ask me for something that I can give you. Ask me for something that I can give you in exchange for the Limbergers' lives."

"Rosalie, you're a fool," the Old One said sharply.

"For once, beast, I agree with you," Blackrose said. "But what she gives me of her own

157

free will, you cannot take away."

"She can't give you her life," the Old One said. "It's not hers to give."

"But her freedom is," Blackrose said. "If the Limbergers are to be spared, she must return, willingly and freely, to her tower, and stay there forever." He turned to the witch. "You, Liederkranz, will never let the golden key out of your sight, so no one will ever open the tower door again." Next, he addressed Rosalie. "If you go back to the tower, I will spare the Limbergers. I have but to ring this bell," he said, pointing to a rope hanging by the side of the fireplace, "and the carrier pigeon will be off."

"Don't do it, Rosalie," the Old One cried. "Don't do it. The Limbergers aren't worth it. You're destined to be queen of the Land of Three Roses. You can't throw your fate away like this."

In a fury, Rosalie turned on the great bear. "You knew!" she cried. "You knew all along who I was. Why didn't you tell me?"

"I didn't know if you were a weakling, like your father," the Old One said. "I didn't know if you were evil, like your uncle. You had to show me you were worthy to rule one day. I think you've done that, so now I can tell you the truth."

Rosalie turned to the Count. "Is this true, Blackrose? Am I truly the heir to the throne of this land?"

158

"Yes," said Blackrose. "You are the heir to the throne I covet. If, as it seems, I must let you live, I wish no one to know that you live—no human being, that is, except my soldiers here who know better than to betray me."

"Then the King at Rosehilde is my father," Rosalie said thoughtfully. It seemed almost worth going back into her tower if she went knowing who she was.

"Yes," said Blackrose, "the King, my older brother, is indeed your father. He's a weak-livered nincompoop. He's not worth having for a father. Why should a mere accident of birth have given him the crown instead of me?"

"If he let you get away with your tyrannies all these years, then I agree he can't be worth much," Rosalie said with a kind of sad pride. "But whatever he is, I needed to know. And my mother? She is the Queen?"

Blackrose nodded. "The Queen, my devoted sister-in-law," he said with a sneer, "from the Land of Seven Lilies, where the whole royal house put together has less guts than I have in my little finger." He waggled his pinkie in Rosalie's face.

Rosalie sighed. "Well, Blackrose," she said, "now I know. Much good it does me." She paused and looked for a moment into those eyes that were so like hers. Then she said, "Just pull that

159

bell rope, and then the Old One will return me to my tower. You won't have to worry about me again."

"Never!" cried the bear. "I won't do it."

"Oh, yes, you will," said Blackrose. "You have to. She goes of her own free will."

"You know what the Old One will do to you if you don't release the Limbergers, don't you?" Princess Rosalie said.

"I would have taken care of you long ago," the bear said, "if that were permitted. But if you betray your bargain with Rosalie, I will forget those rules. I won't care about the consequences."

"I am aware of that," Count Blackrose said. "You don't have to worry."

"The witch will probably help the Old One," Princess Rosalie said. "Won't you, Liederkranz?"

"It wouldn't bother me to see the Count get what he deserves," the witch replied cheerfully. "But I agree with the Old One," she continued. "You're a fool, Princess Rosalie, to give up your freedom for the likes of the Limbergers."

Princess Rosalie did not deign to reply. She climbed up on the bear's back once again. "Ring the bell, Count," she said. "Ring the bell and we'll be off."

The last thing Rosalie saw was the Count give the bell rope a great, hard tug. Then she was surrounded by a deep, cold blackness. She felt the chill, swift air rush by her, and she heard it whistle in their ears. She clutched the Old One around his neck and, shutting her eyes, she buried her face in his fur. She did not look up again until the cold, dark wind had ceased to rush and moan.

She did not know how long the journey had taken, but when she opened her eyes, she saw once again the clear, white light that had always bathed the inside of her tower. She was standing in the middle of her own bedroom. The Count, the witch, the soldiers, even the Old One—they were gone. The sound of silence crushed her ears. She was just as she had been at the beginning—alone, all alone.

Happy birthday to you,
Happy birthday to you,
Happy birthday, dear Rosie,
Happy birthday to you!

It was my birthday. I sang the birthday song a few times to myself before I got out of bed. I figured I'd get in a few choruses just to be safe. The others might not get around to singing me any songs until suppertime.

I decided not to go to school. It was my birthday, after all. If I hung around, you could never tell what might happen.

I woke Dan and then I went downstairs for breakfast in my bathrobe and slippers. As soon as she saw me, Rachel didn't say, "Happy birthday." She said, "Why aren't you dressed?"

"I'm not going to school today. Today is my birthday, in case you forgot."

"Just because it's your birthday is no reason to stay home from school," Rachel replied with a frown.

"I don't feel well," I told her. "I have cramps." Maybe Rachel would understand cramps because she had them sometimes. For good measure I added, "My throat's a little sore, too."

"Well, which is it?" Rachel asked. "A stomach ache or a cold?" From her voice I could tell she didn't believe me.

"Why can't it be both?" I wanted to know.

"If it's both," Rachel said, "it's neither."

"If I go to school and get sick and have to go to the nurse, and the nurse calls up Mom to come and get me, and I tell her you made me go to school, she'll be good and mad."

"But if you don't go to school, and Mother gets up and finds you wandering around in your bathrobe, the perfect picture of good health, she'll be even madder," Rachel pointed out. "She won't like it very much if she has to drive you to school."

"But that'll be my problem," I explained, "not yours. You're not my mother."

That shut her up. She let me finish my breakfast in peace. She and Dan went off to school. I went upstairs and got back into bed. When Mom got up, that's where

I'd be—lying in my bed, my throat getting sorer and sorer. I listened to Don MacNeil and the Breakfast Club on the radio. I read two stories in *The Violet Fairy Book* by Andrew Lang. It was a marvelous book even if I was getting too old for it. It had belonged to Mom when she was a little girl. But I stopped reading after a while. I was tired of lying in bed.

I got up, put my ratty old hand-me-down bathrobe back on, and went downstairs into the kitchen. Olga was in the kitchen too, getting my mother's tray ready. "Ah, Rosie," she exclaimed when she saw me. "You are home. Good. You take up Mama's breakfast. OK? I get it ready. You take it up."

"Not OK," I told Olga.

She was surprised. "But you love to carry up Mama's tray. On Sunday you always bring tray."

"That's Sunday," I pointed out. "Today's Wednesday. I don't know how Mom will take my staying home. I was home two days the week before last."

Just then the telephone rang. There was an extension on the kitchen wall. A pad and pencil hung next to it for messages. Luke answered. "Good morning," he said cheerfully. "Waterbridge Inn." He listened for a moment and then he glanced over at me. The tone of his voice was different when he spoke again. "She isn't feeling well," he said sharply. There was another brief pause. Then he said, "Are you accusing me of lying? Now, listen, lady, what're you bothering with Rosie Gold for? Why don't you go after the kids who aren't getting all A's on their report cards?" Then he slammed the receiver back on the hook.

"What was that all about?" I asked him.

"It was the truant officer at your school," Luke said. "I guess I told her where she could go."

"What was she calling here for?" I wondered. "She's only supposed to call if you're absent three days in a row. I'm never absent three days in a row."

Min came by carrying a pile of tablecloths. "I think maybe they call if you're absent a certain number of days in one month," she said. She had two sons who went to the same school I did. "No matter whether the days are next to each other or not."

"It's all right that I stayed home today, Min, don't you think?" I asked. I was getting a little worried.

Min rested the tablecloths on a tray stand next to the salad bench. "Well, Rosie, I don't know. Are you sick?"

"It's my birthday, Min. Don't you think a person can stay home on her birthday?"

"Well, happy birthday, Rosie," Min said. She turned to Luke. "What do you think, Luke? Do you think it's all right for a person to stay home from school on her birthday?"

"Don't put these big moral questions to me," Luke said. "I'm no good at 'em. All I know, it's plain stupid to come after a child who gets all A's. Let 'em go after the dumb ones. What're they wasting their energy for? And our money."

It was time to change the subject. "Luke," I asked,

"do you know what I'm getting for my birthday? Do you have any idea?"

"Me?" Luke said. "Me? How would I know what you're getting for your birthday? I didn't even know it *was* your birthday."

It wasn't like Luke to forget. He'd remembered other years. He always baked me a cake or some special cookies. "Boy," I said, "everyone's forgetting it's my birthday this year. I wonder if even my mother remembered."

I stalked out of the kitchen and back upstairs to my room. I knelt on the pillow and looked over the headboard of my bed, out the window. I saw the meat man's truck come. I saw the soda man and the egg man and the Schaeffer beer truck. What was I looking for? Maybe a present from God—a stray dog walking up the driveway, a dog so small that even Mom wouldn't mind him. I needed my own dog more than ever. Each day that passed I missed Buster more, not less. The Dunleighs had moved away about a week after Buster died. Mrs. Dunleigh had said the Inn was too full of memories for her, and she couldn't stand living in it any longer. Mom was glad to see her go. She didn't realize that now there was no one for me to even talk about dogs with. Soon Tex would be gone too.

I was thinking about my mother, and then she walked into my room. "Olga told me you were home," she said. "Why aren't you at school? Why aren't you dressed?"

"It's my birthday," I said. "Have you forgotten? It's my birthday."

"Of course I haven't forgotten," Mom replied calmly. "Happy birthday. But your birthday is no reason to stay home from school."

"I don't feel well."

"Rosie . . ." She came over to me, put her hand on my chin, and turned my face toward her. She looked right into my eyes. "Rosie," she said softly, "say that again."

I turned my face away from her. I couldn't say it. Instead I muttered, "I hate school, Mom. I just hate it."

"But you have to go. Get dressed and I'll run you over."

"But what will I say?" I asked desperately. "What will I say when I get there?"

"I'll write a note," Mom replied. "I'll say you over-slept and so did I."

She made me go to school. On my birthday. I was so mad at her I didn't say one word all the way downtown in the car. She said goodbye to me when I got out, but I didn't answer her. That dumb Olga. She had to go tell. She should have kept her mouth shut. Then Mom wouldn't have found out I was home until it was so late it didn't pay anymore to go to school. That's what had happened the week before last. One of the days I stayed home I really had a runny nose. But the other time, Mom hadn't gotten to me until one o'clock in the afternoon.

167

I didn't say much at school either. I was really depressed. None of the other kids in the class knew it was my birthday, because I wasn't having a party. Other years I'd had parties. Not this year. Not for snobs who didn't invite me to their parties. Not for sneak thieves like Bart. I hadn't been able to see the point of a party for any of them except Estelle Coviella, and you can't have just one person at a party. But today I felt different about it. I would have done anything for people to know it was my birthday—anything except tell them. At home, to Rachel or Luke or Min, I could say it was my birthday. But I couldn't say it at school.

At three o'clock I started home. I kind of dragged myself along. I didn't really care when I got there. At supper there'd be a cake and some presents, but not the present I wanted. The day had already been ruined. Whatever happened at supper couldn't save it. I really had to laugh at myself. I had to laugh at all my high hopes that morning. I had stayed home. I had actually stayed home expecting something good to happen.

I had walked about half a mile when I heard Dan calling me. "Rosie, hey, Rosie, wait up." I stopped and turned around. What did he want? Rachel was with him too. They were both running up Queen Street. They seemed to think I might get away from them.

Finally they caught up to me. "What's going on?" I asked. "What's the matter?"

"Oh, nothing," Dan said.

168

"We just wanted to walk home with you," Rachel said. "We saw you walking ahead of us, and we didn't want you to walk alone."

"You must have seen me walking ahead of you a million times," I said, "without ever trying to catch up with me." I was suspicious.

"Don't look a gift horse in the mouth," Rachel said.

"Come on, hurry up," Dan announced. "I want to get home. I've got things to do." He started down the street.

Rachel and I hurried after him. "It's your birthday," Rachel said. "We wanted to walk with you because it's your birthday." That was the first notice anyone had taken of my birthday without a cue from me first. I felt a little better. I was still suspicious, though.

We crossed the highway and started up the long drive. Suddenly Dan muttered, "I just thought of something I've got to take care of right away." He ran up the driveway as if he were being chased by a whole hive of bees.

I looked at Rachel. "What's the matter with him?" I asked.

"He just thought of something he has to take care of," she repeated.

"Oh, come on, Rachel," I protested. "What's the *matter* with him?"

"How do I know?" Rachel sounded annoyed. "Maybe all of a sudden he had to go to the john."

OK, maybe he did. But I doubted it. I started to hurry myself. I wasn't running, exactly, just walking fast.

"Hey," Rachel said, "where're *you* rushing to?"

"Maybe I have to go to the john, too," I said.

"Do you have to do everything he does? Everything?" she asked. "Can't you walk along with me, calmly and sensibly for once, instead of tearing off every which way? After all," she added, "I rushed like the very devil to catch up with you. It isn't so nice of you to go off and leave me all alone."

"All right, all right," I said. "I'll walk with you." And I did. We walked very slowly. I got more and more impatient, but I didn't say anything else about it. When we were almost to the front door. Dan came out. He stood on the low, wide cement stoop in front of the building. He waved at us, and then he ran back inside.

"Boy, Rachel," I said, "you've got to admit he's acting really nuts today. Mostly, from the time he gets up to the time he goes to bed, he hardly even grunts at us. And today he comes out to wave at us? I think all that jazz he listens to is turning his brain to jelly."

"It's your birthday," was all Rachel would say.

We went in through the doors, walked up the cracked marble steps of the foyer, and pushed through the next set of doors. Then we were in the lobby.

Everyone else was in the lobby too. I mean everyone. Mother and Dan and Min and Olga and Luke and Pedro and Tex and Sylvester and Estelle and Cheryl and Bart and even Mr. Neumann, the liquor salesman. Mr. Neumann was holding a small black dog on his lap. "Happy birthday to you," they sang. "Happy birthday to you. Happy birthday, dear Rosie, happy birthday to you." Each voice was at a different place on the scale, but they were loud. Oh, boy, were they loud.

Mom had once told me something funny. She said until I was about four, when they sang "Happy Birthday" to me, I always burst into tears. She said I was embarrassed at being the center of so much attention. If that was true, I'd changed an awful lot. I think I had cried for another reason. Sometimes unexpected happiness hurts so much that you cry.

I stood in the middle of the lobby. I didn't know what to do or say. Mr. Neuman put the little dog down on the floor and got up from the chair he was sitting in. The dog was wearing a bright red collar. Mr. Neumann was holding the end of a red leash. He led the dog over to me and put the leash in my hand. "This is for you," he said. "For your birthday. From your mother."

I found my voice. "Thank you," I said. I knelt down to look at my dog. She was a fuzzy mass of black curls. She could have fit without any trouble at all into a Saltine cracker box. Two button-bright black eyes shone at me. Her pink tongue came out and licked my face. I picked her up in my arms and stood up. "She's a poodle!" I said. "From the litter Bess had a few weeks ago!"

Mr. Neumann nodded. "That's right. She's a full-bred toy poodle." He lowered his voice so only I could hear him. "She's from your mother, you know," he repeated. "I don't give my pups away. They're too valuable for that."

I understood. My mother was standing next to Luke. Still carrying my puppy in my arms, I went over to her and kissed her. "Thank you, thank you," I said. "But I thought you thought an inn was no place for a dog."

"She's a small dog," Mom said, reaching and lightly patting the dog's head. "A very small dog. Max promised she always will be. Right, Max?"

"Right," Mr. Neumann agreed.

"You'll keep her out of the way, won't you, Rosie?" Mom asked. I nodded and the puppy licked my mother's finger. She giggled. "That dog tickles," she said.

"What's my dog's name?" I asked.

"That's for you to decide," Mr. Neumann said. "Don't rush into anything."

"I won't," I agreed.

Then everyone else gave me presents, too. The leash and collar were from Dan and Rachel. Min gave me a box of handkerchiefs. She had embroidered my initial on them. Naturally, Tex gave me three books of fairy tales he had found in a second-hand book store, all by Andrew Lang—*The Green Fairy Book, The Red Fairy Book*, and *The Yellow Fairy Book*. I was getting too old for fairy tales. I wouldn't tell Tex. He would be leaving soon anyway.

Sylvester handed me a box wrapped in silver paper

and tied with wide red ribbon. He didn't say anything as he gave it to me. Sylvester never said anything. Olga spoke for him. "From me, him, and Pedro," she said. "We went together. Get better present that way."

"Thanks," I said. "This is very nice of you. It really is." Olga and Sylvester hadn't given me a present last year. Pedro hadn't either. He hadn't even worked for us last year. It took me a while to undo the wrappings because I had to save them for my mother. Inside the box I found a fuzzy pink sweater. I could see right away it would be too tight. "It's beautiful," I said, "just beautiful." I figured I could exchange it.

Estelle had brought me a little doll dressed in an Italian costume and Bart gave me a huge bottle of toilet water. I guess it cost two dollars. The best present of the three was actually from Cheryl. It was a Monopoly set. Mom must have asked Dan and Rachel which kids to invite, and they had named the ones they'd heard me talk about. I had talked about Millie Van Dyke too, of course, but everyone knew better than to invite her. They shouldn't have invited Bart either, but since he'd brought such a nice present, I let him stay. Mom had rushed downtown as soon as school was out and picked up the kids in the station wagon. We always walked home along Queen Street, so she had met them on Ten Eyk Street. They were a surprise for me. I'd never have believed Bart and Cheryl could keep their mouths shut a whole week the way they had.

After I had opened the presents, all of us except

Luke went into the Holiday Room. We sat at a big round table in the middle of the room. There was a bowl of chrysanthemums in the center, like for a wedding or a banquet. After my mother had arranged us all around the table, Luke came in from the kitchen. He was wheeling one of the big metal carts Min and the other waitresses used to clear parties, and on it was the biggest birthday cake I had ever seen. "This is my present," he said. He must have used garbage can tops for layer pans. "It's all chocolate, inside and out," he added. "I know what my Rosie likes." Everyone sang "Happy Birthday" again, and I blew out all the candles with one enormous breath.

Everyone was kind of quiet while we ate our ice cream and cake and drank Coke. I don't think Estelle, Bart, and Cheryl had ever been at a party before that was mostly grown-ups who weren't even relatives. I had put a big napkin on my lap. My dog was sitting on the napkin. I was so busy watching her, and feeding her cake crumbs when no one was looking, that I didn't talk as much to the kids as I should have.

But then Tex said, "Listen, kids, let's play a game. Let's play Telephone."

"I have work to do," my mother said. She pushed her chair away from the table and got up.

"Me too," Luke and Min said, at the same time.

Tex looked from one of them to the others without smiling. "It can wait," he said. "This game is for everyone."

"You said 'kids,'" Min reminded him.

"Right now, we're all kids," Tex said. "Sit down." So they did, even my mother.

"What's Telephone?" Olga asked. "I never know game called Telephone."

"I'll start," Tex explained. "I'll whisper a phrase in Mrs. Gold's ear." I was sitting next to Tex on one side, and Mom was sitting next to him on the other. "She'll whisper what she thinks she heard to Pedro, and then he'll whisper it to Rachel, and so on, all the way around the table, till it gets to Rosie. She'll tell us what she heard out loud."

"Sounds like a pretty dumb game to me," Luke said.

"It won't seem so dumb when we compare what Rosie says with what I said," Tex told him. He whispered something into my mother's ear, and it went around the table, along with a lot of giggles at each stop. Olga and Bart didn't understand what was said to them, but Tex wouldn't allow repetitions. They just had to pass along what they thought they'd heard. When the message finally got to me, I said, "A hunk of smelly cheese." Everyone got hysterical when they heard that, and they laughed even harder when Tex announced what he'd begun with. It was "Land of Three Roses." We liked the game so much we played it six more times, with different people beginning and ending it each time. I liked Mr. Neumann's message best. It was, "Harry and Bess have a daughter Margaret." It didn't change much as it went around the table, because by then we

175

were all getting much better at listening carefully and whispering clearly. When Dan said the words out loud, they were, "Harry Bates has a doggie Margaret." I knew as soon as I heard him say those words that the pup on my lap was named Margaret.

"Well," my mother said, "this has been a wonderful party, but we really do have to get back to work now. Why don't you kids go up to Rosie's room and play with some of her games? I'll have Min bring you some more refreshments upstairs. Tonight, Rosie, after your dinner, you can take some of this leftover cake around and offer it to customers in the dining room." She came over to me and kissed me. She even patted Margaret again. "Happy birthday, honey," she said. "I'll see you later."

The kids from my class and I went up to my room and played with my new Monopoly set. Rachel played with us too. Bart and Cheryl behaved themselves pretty well. He and I took Cheryl and Estelle on a tour of the place before they went home. They liked that a lot.

I wasn't very hungry at dinner. Neither were Rachel or Dan, even though we ate later than usual. Then, about eight o'clock, I walked around with pieces of chocolate cake to all the tables in the Colonial Room at which people were sitting. I told everyone it was my birthday, and most customers gave me nickels or dimes. I didn't tell Mom about that.

Afterwards, I went back to my room. Margaret was there, waiting for me. I'd put newspapers down all over the floor so she couldn't do any damage if she messed. When I walked in the room, she wagged her tail and ran around me in silly little circles. Already she knew that she was mine and I was hers.

I picked her up and hugged her. Then I sat down at my desk and counted my tips. Ninety-five cents. After all, it had turned into a good birthday.

A week later, Tex left. The day before his last day was a Friday. The three of us spent the whole afternoon in the bar together. Margaret sat on my lap and listened while Tex and I talked about the Land of Three Roses.

*P*rincess Rosalie's tower bedroom was precisely as she had left it not so very long ago—two weeks, perhaps, or three. But it seemed to her that a lifetime had passed, and it was strange that nothing here had changed, when she had changed so much.

But she was too exhausted to wonder about it for very long. She fell onto her bed, fully clothed, and slept.

She slept and slept and slept. When she awakened, there was no way of knowing what time it was. One thing in the tower had changed. Without her there to wind it, the clock had run down. She wandered from room to room, trying to see if anything had been moved, if any dust had gathered, if anything new had been added. But nothing was different—nothing except the run-down clock.

Already she missed everyone terribly. Of course she missed the Old One. That was to be expected. But that she missed Liederkranz and Mr. and Mrs. Limberger and Odora—that was somewhat more surprising. And most surprising of all was the fact that she missed even Count Blackrose's wicked soldiers, and Count Black-rose himself. It had been better before she left the tower. Then she had not known any other kind of life. But now she knew, and even Count Blackrose seemed better than no one at all.

She bathed and changed from her rags into a clean, well-starched gown. She went into the kitchen to see if she could find something to eat. Perhaps food in her stomach would make her feel a little better. She didn't know when the invisible servants would show up—if ever.

As she was rummaging through the cabinets and drawers, in search of a piece of bread or an old potato, a dull roaring sound gradually impressed itself upon her ears. It was the sound of many people shouting. She could not make out what they were saying, but she knew they must be making a great deal of noise and be very close at hand, or else the sound would never have pene-

178

trated the windowless walls of the tower. Such a thing had never happened before.

She left the kitchen, her interest in food forgotten, and made her way to the entryway, where stood the tower's single door, the one that opened only with the great golden key. Princess Rosalie did not expect to see that key again. She was sure it now rested permanently inside Liederkranz's dress, next to her skinny bosom.

In an effort to better hear the noise outside, Princess Rosalie leaned against the door. No sooner did she press against it, than it swung open! For the second time in her life, Princess Rosalie found herself on the green outside the tower. The door no longer needed a key to open it. She could open it herself, with her own strength, her own power.

The shouts rang loud in her ears now. It was her name they were calling, "Rosalie, Rosalie, Princess Rosalie," over and over again. "Princess Rosalie has saved us. Princess Rosalie has saved us."

Gathered on the green before her were nearly all the people she knew—Mr. and Mrs. Limberger and Odora, the Old One, the witch Liederkranz, her daughter Jarlsberg, and Jarlsberg's baby, no longer crying. Hundreds of soldiers dressed in the dark livery of Blackrose stood

179

about, but they carried no weapons. Only the Count himself was missing. There were others too, whom she didn't know, crowds of peasants like the Limbergers, and merchants from the villages and towns. And off to the side, seated on a great gray horse, was a woman dressed in rose-colored velvet trimmed in gold, and wearing on her head a golden coronet. It didn't take any great intelligence to figure out who she was—the Queen herself, come all the way from Rosehilde. Princess Rosalie figured that the Old One must have brought her. Otherwise she could never have come so far so quickly.

The Old One stepped forward and raised his great paws into the air. Instantly the whole crowd fell silent. He bowed low before Princess Rosalie, and she curtsied in return. She wanted to run over and hug him, but she didn't. She had sensed immediately that this was a ceremonial occasion. Certain rules were to be followed. "Hail, Princess Rosalie," he said. "I greet you humbly. All unknowing, you knew more than I did."

Princess Rosalie shook her head. "What did I know, Old One?" she asked. "I knew nothing. I still know nothing."

The Old One made a wide gesture toward the crowd with his hairy arm. "You have saved these people, Princess Rosalie," he said. "You are not only heir to the throne of the Land of Three

180

Roses, you are also the Third Rose, whose coming has broken the power of Blackrose's tyranny."

"I?" Rosalie queried in amazement. "I am the Third Rose?"

"Yes," said Liederkranz as she too stepped closer to Princess Rosalie. "I put my power at Blackrose's disposal years and years ago. My price was gold, gold, gold and more gold. He knew that only the coming of the Third Rose could break his tyranny, but I told him that the Third Rose would be known by its willingness to sacrifice itself for the most humble, the least deserving of Blackrose's people. By this Blackrose thought I meant the Third Rose would never come, for who would make such a sacrifice? I thought I meant that too. It was our secret, his and mine, but he made the mistake of forgetting. If he had not forgotten, he would never have allowed you to buy the Limbergers' lives." She grinned, revealing all three of her black teeth. "You have freed yourself and all the people of County Blackrose. Hail, Princess Rosalie!" Liederkranz curtsied low before her, and then she stepped forward and whispered, "But you don't have to worry about me, Princess Rosalie. I have that gold, all that gold, buried in the Floribunda Forest. Someday soon I may even spend some of it."

At this moment, the great gray horse stepped

181

into the center of the green. Two of the black-uniformed soldiers rushed forward and helped the Queen down from her mount. Princess Rosalie watched in silence. She could not have spoken if she wanted to. There was a great lump in her throat that made speech impossible. As the Queen approached, Rosalie fell to her knees.

The Queen reached out her long white arm and gently lifted Princess Rosalie to her feet. "Do not kneel before me, daughter," the Queen said. "It is I who should kneel before you." Princess Rosalie let out a little cry, and then slapped her hand to her mouth. She recognized the Queen's voice. It was the Voice, her Voice, the Voice that had come to her every day in the tower. "You are the Third Rose," the Queen continued. "You have saved us all." She put her arms around Princess Rosalie and embraced her.

But Princess Rosalie stood within the circle of the Queen's arms as stiff and frozen as an icicle. The Queen dropped her arms and looked at her in dismay. "My daughter, my daughter," she cried, "what's the matter? I am your mother. I have come to you at last—your mother."

"Are you truly my mother?" Rosalie asked.

"Yes," the Queen replied, "truly."

"And are you also the Voice that came to me all those years I was alone?"

"Yes," the Queen replied, "I am."

182

"You could have told me," Rosalie said, her eyes filling with tears. "All those years, I could have known I had a mother. You could have told me."

"Oh, my darling, my darling," the Queen cried, a look of anguish on her exquisite face, "I couldn't. When you were born, Blackrose threatened to have you killed if I didn't let Liederkranz lock you away in a windowless tower. I had to promise not to tell you who you were, or to let anyone else know you hadn't died."

"And you agreed to such a proposal?" Princess Rosalie asked, struggling to control herself as she spoke. "You are my mother, and you agreed?"

"Don't be so hard on me, Rosalie," the Queen begged. "I had no choice. Can't you see that? I had no choice. I managed to persuade Liederkranz to let me come to you two hours every day. I had to give her every precious thing I owned to win that much."

Princess Rosalie seemed scarcely to hear her. "And my father—the King—he was willing to consign me to such a fate?" she continued relentlessly.

The Queen nodded sadly. "He's not a strong man, Rosalie."

"That," the Old One interrupted harshly, "is the best that can be said of him."

The Queen turned to the Old One. "It's not for

183

you to judge him," she said sharply. "What do you know of human beings, after all? The King was completely in Blackrose's hands. He promised to make Blackrose his heir, and hide the true heir away, if Blackrose would just let him sit on the throne at Rosehilde as long as he lived. You know that if he hadn't made such an agreement, Blackrose would have destroyed him long ago. But since the King is so much older than Blackrose, Blackrose was willing to wait a while, for the sake of the appearance of legitimacy. And the King hoped the Third Rose would appear in time to save us all. Maybe he did more than hope. Maybe he *knew*."

"I can't believe it," Princess Rosalie said. "I cannot believe it. I have a mother and a father who conspired with my greatest enemy to shut me up in a tower. I think it would have been better to have no mother and father at all." She walked slowly toward the Old One and looked up into his strong, proud face. "I wish you were my father, Old One," she said. "It was you who found the key to my tower and put it in my drawer, wasn't it?"

"Yes," said the Old One, "it was me. I had never approved of their locking you up in the first place. If the King and Queen had asked my advice, as they certainly should have, I would have told them to look for a better way."

"But when she got out," the Queen said, "it was I who arranged for her safekeeping at the Limbergers, in a place obscure enough to hide her from Blackrose's sight. Don't forget that, Old One!"

"And who saw to it that the stream took her there?" the Old One asked with a sniff. "Blackrose nosed her out anyway," he added, "because someone at Rosehilde couldn't keep his—or her—mouth shut. I wonder who," he scowled at the Queen.

"Stop quarreling," Princess Rosalie ordered suddenly. "It sounds so silly for two old things like you to be fighting with each other. What's done is done."

Her mother put her hand out and touched the Princess's shoulder. "Do you really believe that, Rosalie?" she asked.

"You each did what you thought was right," Princess Rosalie admitted. "No one can do anything more than that. You want to love me. I want to love you. I do. Really, I do." She stood on her tiptoes and kissed them on the cheek, first the Queen and then the Old One, and as she did this, the crowd let out a great cheer.

"Then you forgive me?" the Queen asked. "You forgive me for letting Liederkranz put you in the tower?"

"Don't ask for too much, Mother," the Princess

said. "Let's start from where we are." But she smiled a little as she said it, and linked her arm through her mother's. "I always knew," she added softly, "I always knew that my Voice loved me."

Princess Rosalie, the Old One, and the Queen went back inside the tower. Liederkranz and the Limbergers came too. They had hot coffee with warm milk and sweet buns for breakfast, and they sat talking all the rest of the morning.

They didn't live happily ever after. Life went on, with bad times and good ones. Rosalie didn't mind. It would have been boring any other way.

"That's the end, Rosie," Tex said. "It has to be. To-morrow's my last day."

"The end for now," I said. "Maybe some day, some place, there'll be some more."

"Oh, there's more all right," Tex agreed. "Whether we both know about it or not, there's always more."

I stood up and leaned all the way over the bar. "Goodbye, Tex," I said.

He kissed me on the cheek. "Goodbye, Rosie, dar-ling," he said.

I walked out of the bar carrying Margaret in my arms. I got my coat and then I took her outside. I ran with her, and jumped with her, and played ball with her for a long, long time. It was the end of December,

187

the end of the year. Black night fell early, and the green neon sign on the roof flashed on, and so did all the street lamps in the parking lot. It was cold out, bitter cold. Margaret and I went back into the worn-out, warm old building for supper.

BARBARA COHEN is the author of *The Carp in the Bathtub, Thank You, Jackie Robinson, Where's Florrie?, Bitter Herbs and Honey, Benny,* and *The Binding of Isaac.* A former teacher and a newspaper columnist, she lives in a small town in New Jersey with her husband Gene and their three daughters, Leah, Sara, and Rebecca.

F
COH

160

Cohen, Barbara

R, my name is Rosie

DATE DUE
